AUG 1 0 2021

THE HALLOWEEN MOON

THE
HALLOWEEN
MOON

JOSEPH FINK

Quill Tree Books
An Imprint of HarperCollinsPublishers

Quill Tree Books is an imprint of HarperCollins Publishers.

Library of Congress Control Number: 2021935342
ISBN 978-0-06-302097-9

Typography by Catherine San Juan
21 22 23 24 25 PC/LSCH 10 9 8 7 6 5 4 3 2 1
❖
First Edition

To Leaf, Caleb, Olsen, Elliette, and Iris.

THE HALLOWEEN MOON

BEFORE

THE BENNINGTON MUSEUM of the Unusual and Rare was not an attraction that received many visitors. Most people had no idea it existed, which was exactly how the museum wanted it.

The only regular visitor was James Bennington, who was also its owner and curator. He had put the greater part of a vast inheritance into it, and so he felt entitled to his nightly private tours, given only to himself, smirking proudly at his trophies.

Other than James, the most frequent visitors were those delivering new items to the collection. As a courtesy, he would usually show them around, although even then he would keep back some of the more rare and famous pieces. It was better that no one knew about those. And he also took care on such tours to emphasize and demonstrate the scale and severity of the security systems in the building. Given the occupation of these visitors, and the temptation that his collection represented, it was wise to make clear up front that any attempt to steal from him would end abruptly and poorly.

Once in a great while, he would have a friend in the museum, a fellow collector of the priceless. These occasions were rare because James had almost no friends. He liked to think that his collection was all the friend he needed. But if a collector of his caliber visited, he would give a tour on the understanding that this would be reciprocated later with a tour of the visitor's collection. These were the only people James allowed to see the rarest pieces, partly to show them that he had definitely outdone them with his collection, and partly so that when he visited them, they would not hold anything back from him. There was an understanding among collectors such as he. They did not live ordinary lives, nor did they follow ordinary rules. They were better than that, and the scale of their collections was proof of their extraordinary natures.

The Bennington Museum of the Unusual and Rare showed up in no guidebooks and had no reviews on the internet. It was not registered with any organization. In fact, to the world, it was not a museum, but simply James's house, tucked safely away behind walls and gates and security cameras on a nondescript cul-de-sac in one of the many hillsides of Southern California settled by the wealthy and famous.

James was not famous, had no interest at all in fame. Many of his neighbors were celebrities, and this only annoyed him, since it meant that cars and tour buses came by to look at the neighborhood where this actor or this sports star or whatever lived. He didn't care about who his neighbors were. He only cared about his collection, and the absolute privacy of himself and his visitors.

The reason he detested publicity was simple: his collection was not legal. Every item in it had been stolen, from museums mostly, or heavily guarded storage facilities, or sometimes from the homes of other collectors, although very rarely, because of course stealing from a fellow collector was only an invitation for them to steal from you. The illegal collecting community was built on a mutual trust that was, in turn, built on a mutual distrust.

On this particular night in early October, an uncomfortably dry and warm fall evening, with the wind whipping hot and fast in from the desert, spreading a fire through the hills so the air was smoky and palpable even in this cloistered little neighborhood, miles from danger, James was expecting no visitors at all. Even a minute outside in these conditions left him choking and wiping at his eyes, so he had spent the day tucked safely away in the filtered and conditioned air of his museum.

All to say that he was confused and frightened when there was a knock at the door. No one should have even been able to knock on his door, since it was behind a secure fence and past several sensors and cameras. But there was definitely a knock. He pulled out his phone and texted his chief of security, Donna. He had an on-site security staff at all times, and Donna herself practically lived at the house, overseeing its protection. She responded to any texts within seconds, twenty-four hours a day. But Donna did not reply to the text. Minutes passed with no reply. The knocking continued.

He went to the intercom and flicked it on. "Go away," he said, in a voice he incorrectly thought sounded brave. "There is armed security on its way. If you leave now, we won't press charges."

"That's not very welcoming at all," a voice from close behind him said.

He screamed and whirled around. There was a man wearing a uniform like an old-fashioned diner waiter, black pants and white shirt, and a white paper hat. Every part of his outfit was perfectly pressed and neatly maintained.

"Oh, I'm sorry, I didn't mean to scare you," the man said. He smiled, a warm and utterly false smile. "It's only that no one was answering my knocking."

"The police are on their way," James said. "You need to leave."

"The police?" the man said. "But you said it was armed security. Which is it, Mr. Bennington?"

James heard a skittering sound. Like a swarm of insects. And was that a child who just ran down the hallway behind the man? It had looked like a child. No children had ever been allowed in the museum. He shuddered to think what a child might do to a collection like his.

"No one is on their way, Mr. Bennington, are they?" the man said. He didn't come any closer, leaning on the mantelpiece of one of the house's eight fireplaces. "And you are fine. You are totally fine. We merely need one item from your collection."

"My collection is not for sale."

The man's smile got wider. Hungrier. "We aren't buying."

This time three children most definitely ran down the hall. They were wearing ragged and dirty Halloween costumes, although it wouldn't be Halloween for another three weeks. One, dressed like a pirate, turned to look at James as they ran by, but the light flickered oddly and he couldn't see the child's face.

"I have a security staff at all times," James said. "They have the house surrounded."

"Oh?" the man said, looking around with a gleeful performance of curiosity. He examined the complete lack of other people in the vicinity, and then listened to the utter absence of approaching footsteps outside. He held up his hands, a pose that said, *What are you going to do? Good help is hard to find.*

"I'm sure it's as you say, sir," the man said. "And while it's true I myself don't have a security staff to match the one that is undoubtedly on its way to arrest us, what I do have"—and here he unfolded one long, pale finger to indicate behind James—"is her."

The woman was in the doorway behind him. She hadn't

been there before, and he was sure he hadn't heard her approach. She was simply not there and then there. Pure power radiated from her. She was small, but her shadow stretched strangely across the room, far too long for her diminutive human form.

"Hey there, sorry!" the woman said, scrunching her face apologetically. "This won't take a sec, and then we'll be totally out of your hair. Promise. I know I certainly hate unexpected visitors. Come on, Dan."

The peculiar man and the terrifying woman turned and walked down the hall toward the collection. James, despite his fear, hurried after them. No matter who these weirdos were, he would never let anyone touch his collection.

But, to his horror, they already were. There were filthy, costumed children crawling all over the place, like an elementary school Halloween party, sitting inside cases that he had been assured were completely theft-proof, curiously picking up ancient urns and putting handprints on pieces of Renaissance art registered in international databases as "Permanently Lost." It was his worst nightmare.

The woman and her paper-hatted sidekick ignored the children and walked through the collection with a focused intent.

"As we were told," the woman said, stopping at one particular case. "Exactly what we needed."

James flapped his arms frantically.

"Absolutely not. That statue is priceless. The artist died while carving it. You can see where he chipped the elbow as he collapsed. There have been entire books written about that statue. There is no piece of art like it in the country. In the world."

The paper-hatted man casually lifted the theft-proof plexiglass case, like it was the cover on the scrambled eggs at a free hotel breakfast.

"Don't worry, sweetheart," said the woman with the strange shadow. "I've no interest in the statue. See?"

Like a cat knocking a glass off a table, she playfully scooted the statue to the edge of the display while James's guts twisted, and then the statue fell and shattered. James couldn't breathe. He would rather she had killed him. His collection was more than him. It was his legacy to the world, although he would never let the world see it.

The woman laughed, and he knew then that she was not a woman. She was some seething, deep power, wearing the flimsy costume of a human, as false as the costumes on all these children that had somehow gotten into his museum. It was like the sun had put on a plastic dollar-store mask and strolled about the earth, pretending to be a person.

"What I want," the woman said, "is this." She picked up what had been next to the statue and tossed it lightly from hand to hand.

"That?" James said, when he found air again. "But that's . . . I mean, in a collection like this . . . it has some interest, but it barely has value outside of the novelty . . ."

"Perfect!" the woman said. "Then you won't even miss it. It'll be like we weren't even here."

And just then they weren't. James was once again alone with his collection. No children, no paper-hatted man, and no woman who was not a woman.

He looked around and assessed the damage. The statue was unrecoverable, and that hit him in the guts all over again. And of course there was the theft of the trinket. But his museum was sprawling, with countless rare, one-of-a-kind items. All in all, he had made it through this okay. Terrified but okay. He put one hand on his chest, felt the air going in and out of his body, and let his racing heart settle back down to its usual pace.

Which was when he heard the sound that had haunted his dreams for years. The wail of police sirens in his front drive.

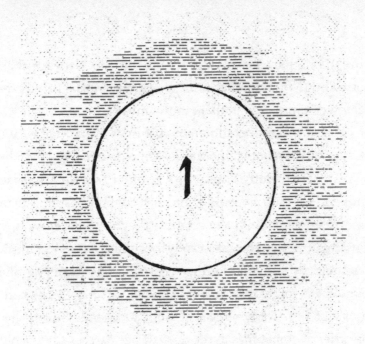

1

ESTHER GOLD LOVED HALLOWEEN.

Maybe you love Halloween. Maybe you dress up every year and put a lot of time and care into your costume. Maybe you watch scary movies and then can't sleep but also can't resist watching more. Maybe candy corn tastes better to you than other candy not because it tastes better (it doesn't) but because it tastes like a moment in time, like a season.

But you don't love Halloween the way Esther did.

Esther refused to watch anything that wasn't a scary movie. Her dad liked to watch sitcoms. Her mom liked to watch important dramas starring important people. Her brother liked watching movies in which people kissed, although he pretended he didn't. But Esther only liked movies with darkness and Dutch angles and the part where the main character leans down to the sink to wash their face and then when they look up again there is a pale, menacing creature behind them in the mirror.

Esther made three different costumes every Halloween. One was for school. One was for trick-or-treating. And one was in case the other two didn't turn out as well as she had hoped. She put more time into her backup costume than most people put into any costume they would ever wear.

Esther didn't even like candy, but she collected as much as she possibly could for the sheer act of collecting it. She would eat some of it, sure, it was fine, but mostly the contents of her overflowing bag went to friends and to her brother or sometimes to the trash, if her parents discovered how much candy she had managed to collect.

"Unhealthy," her father often said. He was right.

"Greedy," her mother often said. She was wrong.

Esther wasn't greedy about the candy. She didn't collect it merely to have it. She collected it because it was part of the ritual of Halloween, and more than anything, she loved this annual night when everyone gave up on being realistic, and clearheaded, and being too old for scary stories, and just let themselves pretend a little.

This is what Halloween was to Esther. It was a night in which the whole neighborhood came together to tell a story, and, above all, Esther loved stories.

Yes, Esther Gold loved Halloween. But one year, Halloween was not a holiday about getting together to pretend a scary story. One year, the scary story became real.

10

2

ESTHER HAD ALWAYS BEEN the only Jewish kid in her grade. This had usually not mattered to her. Being Jewish wasn't that big of a deal anymore, she would tell herself. But also it mattered a lot. It was both important and unimportant at the same time.

If she had been asked to explain this, she wouldn't have been able to, but she felt it.

When she was eight, she and all the other kids she had grown up with had moved to a new school. They were leaving the school for the little kids and going to the school where they would be staying through junior high. It was a defining moment, as far as such terms apply in towns where not a lot ever happens.

The first day of school had been on Yom Kippur. No one who set the calendar for the school district knew they had scheduled it this way. They didn't know what Yom Kippur was.

As the other kids got to know their new school, Esther spent the day in her synagogue, which was a thirty-minute drive from the town she lived in. When she arrived on the second day of school, everyone else knew where the bathrooms were, where to go for recess and lunch, and all of the new rules that had been explained to them while she was at synagogue. It felt like vertigo. Her hands shook, and she couldn't make them stop.

The teachers did their best to help her out, but none of them were very sympathetic. None of them could understand why she didn't just show up to the first day of school.

Her grandmother had been the one who taught Esther to love her Jewish identity, to be proud of it even if perhaps people treated her worse because of it. Her grandmother's name was Debbie, and Esther's parents would have named her after Debbie, except that Jewish people don't name children after people who are still alive, so Esther had been named after her great-grandmother instead. It was Debbie who had first introduced Esther to a love of Halloween. Esther's parents didn't get it, but Debbie would have Esther over when she was little, take her trick-or-treating, and show her spooky movies probably a touch too old for her at the time.

Now Esther was thirteen. Her bat mitzvah had been four months earlier. It was Halloween themed of course, even though it was in June, which the kids at her synagogue would have found incredibly dorky if she had invited even a single one of them. They were all from the same town, which wasn't her town, and so it felt like all of them were already friends with each other. There had never been room for her to join their close-knit cliques. And so while they invited each other to their bar and bat mitzvah parties, she only invited her family and a few non-Jewish friends from school. It was okay. The party ruled. She had a magician perform. She loved magicians for the same reason she loved Halloween; they told a story that promised a world more interesting than the world she had to live in. Grandma Debbie had loved it. The rest of the adults were less sure.

"You know," her dad had said at the party, looking over the paper cut-out bats and ghosts on the wall, "this means you're an adult now. And adults don't go trick-or-treating."

She had ignored that, and it hadn't come up again since. She knew that eventually there would come a last year she could go door to door, walking past a few plastic pumpkins scattered half-heartedly on a lawn or past elaborate front yard displays full of fake body parts and light-up ghosts. There would come a last year she would feel that moment of anticipation and apprehension as she knocked on a stranger's door and waited to see who would answer. There would come a last year for the satisfying weight of a full bag of candy after a round of trick-or-treating. But this was not that year. Next year maybe. Or the year after. Or the year after that.

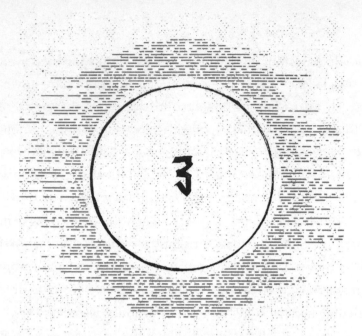

ON THE DAY BEFORE HALLOWEEN, Esther started her walk home from school by herself. Her parents let her walk alone because their house was only ten minutes away from the school, and the roads between were all quiet and suburban. Still, many of her friends' parents gawped in horror as they watched her go right past the waiting line of SUVs and minivans in the school parking lot, shocked to see her step out onto a public sidewalk rather than get into an air-conditioned vehicle.

Sasha Min's mother called, "Do you want a ride, honey?" And Sasha groaned from the back, where she was sitting next to her brother, Edward, in his car seat.

"No, Mom, not her."

"Sasha, do not be a brat. Esther, honey, it's dangerous to walk alone. Hop in."

"That's okay, Mrs. Min," she said, and Sasha sighed in loud relief.

"I don't know what your parents are thinking, letting you walk all that way by yourself," Mrs. Min said, just loud enough that Esther could hear. Edward threw one of his toy trucks from the back seat into the front seat and laughed.

Esther didn't get the big deal. It was a ten-minute walk. She didn't know what kind of great dangers Mrs. Min thought might be lurking in the lazy sunlight of a Southern California afternoon, but the most threatening obstacles Esther had ever encountered during the day were those same parents, too busy scolding their children while driving to notice Esther crossing the street.

The way home wound by a series of quiet cul-de-sacs before dipping through a bit of wild land that had been left by the real estate developer as a combination vacant lot and low-maintenance park. The truth was that the developer hadn't wanted to shell out the money for bulldozing the little canyon into submission. And so there was this pit of land full of narrow trails, some put there half-heartedly by the developer and some etched by the eager feet of children as they sought out every hidden cranny and secret clearing. The stream that ran though the center of the canyon was just gutter runoff on its way to the city sewer.

When the sun was out, the canyon was a playground for the neighborhood's children, and Esther loved it for the adventure it offered, only a short and steep dirt path down from a suburban street. But the moment the sun went down, the safety of the canyon disappeared, and it became the domain of all sorts of creatures, from roving coyotes to, most worrisome of all, high schoolers who were known to use the secluded areas of the canyon for late-night parties. The canyon was where the older teenagers did whatever they couldn't do in the streets and empty parking lots. Esther was wisely cautious of the feral animals, but it was the older kids and their parties, parties that felt to her both grown-up and wild, that put a pit in her stomach as big as the canyon itself.

As she walked home that afternoon, the canyon was still in its daylight form, a pretty bit of nature between tract homes. She took the path through the center of the canyon, across the wooden bridge over the gray gutter runoff pretending to be a stream, past the low-hanging branches of a white flowered plant she knew was called "mule fat." (This plant and its name are real. Look it up.) Her father had taught her the name on one of their walks when she was little, and it had always stuck with her, even as she had forgotten every other plant he had taught her.

Past the mule fat was a tunnel that went under the main road. The walls of the tunnel were made of corrugated metal, so passing though it made her feel like water running down a drain. In the middle of the tunnel the air got cold, no matter how warm the day. It was the only part of the walk home that Esther found unnerving. The shadows in the middle of the tunnel were deep, seeming to promise secret side passageways leading even farther away from the warmth of day, passageways that a child would never find their way out of.

She and her friend Agustín had grown up playing in the canyon. They had made up a game called "The Feats of Strength." One of them would announce that the game was starting, and then they both had to get through a series of feats before the other did.

The first feat was climbing to the top of the tunnel entrance and sitting with your feet dangling over. Then, you had to crawl through a narrow pipe in the drainage ditch. Third, you made your way carefully (and often painfully) up a steep slope covered in cactus, running along a secret path that the two of them had formed by passing over it so many times (the path was directly against the back fences of nearby houses, and the dogs in those backyards would jump and bark as they ran), to the site of the final and as yet unattempted feat. This was leaping from a ledge into a pond full of runoff water below. Neither of them had ever completed that last feat, mainly because the height of the jump scared them both, but also, and this was the reason they said out loud and chose to believe, the pond was absolutely disgusting; brackish, algae covered, and full of who knows what from the city gutters.

But Agustín wasn't with her on this walk, so she hurried through the tunnel to the other side, where the trail grew broad and flat, winding along the fake stream until it rose sharply back up to the gate that led to her street. She came out of the gate and turned the corner, passing Mr. Nathaniel's house.

Mr. Nathaniel was washing his car. He washed his car constantly, even though there was usually a drought declared in Southern California. And he never seemed to drive it anywhere, so the car never got dirty. It was a Ford pickup, stationed always in the driveway. Not only did Mr. Nathaniel hose it down a couple times a week, but he also liked to spray down his driveway and the sidewalk in front of it. It drove Esther's father crazy.

"We're in a water shortage, and he's watering the side-walk," her father would say, peeking through the blinds of their front window at Mr. Nathaniel, who was stubbornly spraying the concrete like it might sprout and grow.

Once, Mr. Nathaniel had even gone out in the middle of a rainstorm, standing outside without an umbrella or jacket, his shirt clinging and turning see-through, spraying water onto a driveway that had already become a waterfall after two days of rain. That time Esther's father had been too angry even to speak.

"I . . . ," he had said to Esther, waving his hand. "Well . . . ," he had said, and then he had gone to take a nap. Sometimes when Esther's father got too frustrated, he would just take a nap.

Esther didn't like Mr. Nathaniel. Not for the same rea-son as her father. She also thought that his constant car and sidewalk washing were wasteful, but the real reason she didn't like Mr. Nathaniel was because there was an aspect about him that unsettled her. Nothing specific, but on a gut level, he didn't feel right. She hated walking by his house when he was outside, which he often was, hair mussed, wrinkled face sullen and blank, checkered shirt loose at the collar with a white tuft coming out of it at his throat. As long as she could remember he had seemed the same age, and that age was very old.

She walked quickly past him. He ignored her and kept spraying his car, although she swore that he aimed the hose intentionally so the water bounced off its side and sprayed her. Now her socks and shoes were all wet. She hated Mr. Nathaniel.

Two doors down from Mr. Nathaniel was the Gabler house. The Gablers were perfectly nice people except for one great crime that outweighed every pleasant "Oh, hi there, Esther" and friendly wave. The crime was this: Mr. Gabler was a dentist, and so on Halloween night, they put out a bowl full of toothbrushes and toothpaste tubes.

Esther didn't require that everyone love Halloween as much as she did. She didn't require that everyone participate. Some people turned off their lights and pretended they weren't home when Halloween came around, and that was fine with her. As long as there were always some houses with lights on and jack-o'-lanterns lit, then the nonparticipators were merely background noise to her Halloween experience.

But to actively spit in the face of all that Halloween stands for by getting every passing trick-or-treater's hopes up, only to have those hopes dashed by a plastic bowl full of what could only be described as the moral opposite of candy? This to Esther was a crime without pardon. Her only solace was that the toothbrushes usually ended up scattered all over their lawn, and the toothpaste tubes were often put on the Gablers' front walk and stomped until they exploded, a little mint rainbow on the concrete, left to dry to a chalky lump by the next morning's sun. Once a year, on November first, Mr. Gabler looked like Mr. Nathaniel, carefully going over his driveway with a hose.

"Oh, hi there, Esther," called Mr. Gabler. He often came home for lunch, since his office was only a ten-minute drive away. Right now, it looked like he was on his way back to his car for an afternoon of rooting around in people's mouths.

"Hi, Mr. Gabler," she said, trying to sound as pleasant as she possibly could. She knew his heresy against Halloween wasn't really his fault. He just didn't get it. She could, and did, and always would forever and ever, hold it against him, but she still tried to be polite about it. In any case, the truth was that the toothpaste wasn't what bothered her most about Mr. Gabler. The main issue was his absolute mundanity. There was no adventure that she could see to his life, and it seemed such a waste of the freedom adulthood gives you to spend it staring in strangers' mouths and watching TV news every night. It was the opposite of everything Halloween stood for to Esther. The toothpaste was only a symptom of the utter boredom of Mr. Gabler's life.

"Say hello to your dad for me," Mr. Gabler said as he got back into his car.

"I sure will," she said, to the slamming of his car door. She sure wouldn't. Toothpaste. Ugh.

As she reached her corner, she heard strange music in the air. She had never heard music like it before. It was the warbling chime of an ice cream truck, but the melody wasn't any of the happy and annoying melodies those trucks usually blared. Instead, the music sounded sad, or even angry. The song was complex and long, and a little off-key. It was the music an ice cream truck would play at a funeral, if anyone was ever eccentric enough to have an ice cream truck at their funeral.

The source of the music came trundling out of the cul-de-sac with worn tires and a hood belching puffs of black smoke. The ice cream truck, if that's what it was, was filthy, and along the side of the truck there was the faded image of a jack-o'-lantern, drawn so crudely that it barely resembled any jack-o'-lantern she had ever seen. In chipped and badly applied type around the jack-o'-lantern were the words "Queen of Halloween Pumpkins. Get yours while they last!"

An ice cream truck that sold pumpkins. What an odd idea, but she also found it cool. More everyday institutions should be changed in October to celebrate Halloween. Schools should teach ghost stories. Every house should be haunted. Every dream should be a nightmare.

The driver gave her a long look as he drove by. His hair was greasy and combed down over his face. What she could see of his expression looked sullen, like he hated not only his job, but the whole world too. Suddenly the idea of the truck seemed less cool. She decided it was best to get through her front door, and quick.

By the time she got inside and up to her room, she was already forgetting about the creepy man driving the ice cream truck that wasn't an ice cream truck. Because it was only one more night until Halloween, and there was so much left to do.

"ESTHER!" HER DAD SHOUTED.

"Esther!" her mom shouted.

"Oh, you wanted to talk to her too?" her dad said.

"You go first," her mom said.

"No, no, please."

"Esther, I want to talk about Halloween."

"Oh! That's what I wanted to talk to her about too."

"We should have discussed this beforehand, shouldn't we?"

Sometimes her parents were so helpless at parenting that she loved them all the more for it. They had three children, with her in the middle, and they still hadn't figured out conversations like this.

Continuing to chatter away nervously about their lack of plan, her parents sat her down by the grand piano in the living room. Her dad led a wedding band for a living, and so he had instruments of all kinds scattered throughout the house. This week he had found a used saxophone online and was trying to teach himself to play it, much to the dismay of everyone else in the house, even Esther's three-year-old sister, Sharon. Each family member had their own way of expressing this displeasure. Her mom smiled even more than she regularly did, but her smile had a lot more teeth than usual. Esther's older brother was always over at his friends' houses, whiling away sunny California afternoons in dark bedrooms playing video games for five or six hours at a time. Her sister threw tantrums and cried about Daddy's new fart horn. And Esther expressed herself the same way she expressed herself about anything: by preparing even more seriously for Halloween.

"Esther, we know how much you love Halloween," her mom said.

They didn't, though. Oh, they understood that she liked it a lot—clearly they detected a real affinity for the holiday. But they did not understand how for her the year revolved around the end of October the way it does for other kids around Christmas or summer vacation or their birthday.

"And we're glad to see you excited about something," her dad said. "Excitement is . . . exciting."

Her parents didn't seem to know who should say what. Her mom paused for her dad to jump in, and then he didn't, so she started to talk just as he noticed the pause and started to talk and they both spoke at once and then paused.

Finally her mom said, "Esther, you're thirteen now. You've had your bat mitzvah. You're an adult."

"Mom, I think both of us know that I'm not really an adult."

"You are in some ways," her dad said. "You're getting there. And being an adult doesn't mean you have to give up being excited about hobbies. Look how excited I've been about learning the saxophone."

Her mom and Esther grimaced in unison.

"But," her dad continued without noticing, "it does mean that you have to think about how your hobbies affect others."

"Yes, yes," her mom said, nodding at her dad with real annoyance. "*Everyone* in this house should think about how their hobbies affect others."

"Exactly," her dad said, satisfied that finally he and her mom were on the same page.

Her mom was a court reporter, a job she despised but tolerated. The pay was decent, as were the hours, and so she constantly said that she had no reason to complain. She would say that again and again, until it started to sound to Esther a lot like complaining. And her mom was not particularly sympathetic to Esther's creative excesses around Halloween.

Her dad, being someone who played music for a living, should have been more understanding. But working in a creative field only made him constantly aware of how much basic business sense and wild luck were required to turn an artistic pursuit into a job, and so in many ways he was more serious than her mom.

"Anyway, this has maybe gotten away from us a bit," her mom said. "I don't know if you've noticed, but we're not always good at stuff like this."

"Oh?" said Esther.

"But it comes down to this, Est," her dad said. "We think maybe this is the year you don't go trick-or-treating."

Her heart made a move she had never felt before. Like it had shrunk but also relocated somewhere into her knees.

". . . what?" she whispered. Her voice didn't sound like her. Who was that hoarse and timid weakling using her mouth to speak?

"Oh, honey," her mom said. "I know you love trick-or-treating, but that's something for children to do. And you're not a child anymore. That doesn't mean you have to stop having fun! Maybe you could answer the door in your costume. Give candy to the kids. It might be fun to be on the other side of that equation for the first time."

"Or we could have a little Halloween dinner. Make pumpkin cupcakes or something," her dad said.

Esther felt that she needed to lie down. This was horrible.

"Whatever you do tomorrow," her mom said, "we just think it's time you stopped trick-or-treating. It's not fair to the kids who are young enough to do it, and people are going to start being, well, weirded out when a teenager shows up at their door asking for candy."

"I'm not a teenager!"

"You are, though," her dad said. "Believe us, we're no happier about it than you are."

26

"Okay," she said, looking for some angle to bargain with, "I see what you're saying, and I understand. This will be the last year I go trick-or-treating. It will be hard, but you're right. After this year, I'll be done." She didn't mean any of that. She would be right out there next year, but it would give her twelve whole months to figure out how to work around her parents.

"No, honey, you're not hearing us," her mom said. "Last year was the last year. You're not going trick-or-treating this year. This isn't optional."

"I hate you!" she shouted. That wasn't what she meant to say. She didn't hate them. But she couldn't believe they were doing this to her, and she didn't know what other words to use to communicate that utter disbelief. Lately she had been feeling more emotions than she had words to express, and if that was what being a teenager was, then count her out on that.

"Esther," her dad said, shaking his head in disappointment.

"You don't hate us," her mom said. "You also shouldn't make strong statements like that if you don't mean them."

"I do!" she said. "I do hate you." She didn't hate them. She didn't even know why she was saying it, but she couldn't stop herself.

"Alright, hate us," her dad said. "You're not going trick-or-treating either way. That part isn't your choice. Your choice is if you want to be angry and miserable about it, or have a good night instead."

"Honey, listen, you can still do something fun," her mom said. "We're going to let this tantrum you're throwing right now slide because we know how hard this is for you."

"We are?" her dad said to her mom. "We do?"

"Yes, we do and we are. Oh! I know. Why don't you go with Agustín and his mom to the movies?"

Of course. That was it. Agustín would be her way out of this. She forced herself to smile, take a few breaths. She wanted to trick-or-treat, and so she would. Her parents' wishes would not get in the way of her own.

"You're right, Mom, Dad. I'm sorry I said all that." She wasn't sorry. "I'll call Agustín and see if I can go with them. Thanks for suggesting it."

She got up and walked to her room. Her mom and dad looked at each other, trying to figure out if they had done the parenting thing correctly there or not.

"That probably went as well as it could," her mom said.

"Think she's going to try to sneak out and go anyway?" her dad said.

"Ha! Yeah. Yes. Definitely."

In her room, Esther pulled up her most recent text chat. She and Agustín had been best friends for years.

"Hey, we need to talk," she typed. "You around?"

"Sure. Cool. Want me to head over?"

"No, I'll come to you. See you in five."

She stood to leave, already planning the act of contrition she would put on for her parents. As she stood, movement caught her eye outside her window. There was a group of trick-or-treaters walking down the street. It was the day before Halloween. What were they doing out there? And why were a bunch of little kids like that walking around without an adult?

One was dressed as a ghost, white sheet and eye holes and all. One was dressed as a pirate. One was dressed as a witch. Their costumes were filthy and torn. Who had let them outside in old costumes that were in such bad condition? The pirate turned to look at her, as if they knew she was watching. She couldn't see the child's face. They were standing in bright afternoon sunlight, and there should have been no shadows from that angle. But she couldn't see their face. The pirate looked away, and the small, ragged group of trick-or-treaters continued around the corner and out of sight. Esther Gold felt a cold fear run through her body, and she didn't know why.

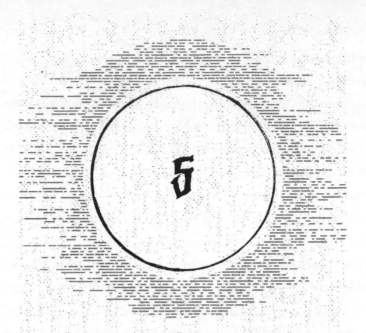

"HEY," AGUSTÍN SAID, from among the gravestones. The gravestones did not mark any graves. His mother carved them for a living in a workshop out back of the house, and she put them on the front lawn as an advertisement for her business. The climbing vines on the side of the house grew out through the gravestones, giving the whole yard a wild air. As a result, their yard got a lot of interest during Halloween. No one in Agustín's family liked Halloween.

Agustín lounged on a beach chair set up between an old-school raised gravestone and a more earthquake-safe, flat-to-the-ground slab. Both of the gravestones were marked with the word "Sample," which made the whole yard look like the last resting place for a family named Sample. The beach chair was always out between the graves in the front yard. When Agustín's grandfather had first immigrated to the United States, he had ended up in Michigan, which is where Agustín's mom grew up. When she had moved her family to Southern California, the winter warmth had been not merely a novelty but a true miracle to her. She reveled in short sleeves in December and liked to sit out in a beach chair and chat with the neighbors in the afternoons as people returned from school and work.

"Listen, Gus," Esther said. "I need a favor."

"What kind of favor?"

She and Agustín had been friends since second grade, when random seat assignments had put them at the same desk. After a couple days of playful bickering, they had become inseparable and remained that way. They played video games and wandered around in the canyon, exploring and developing the challenges that would become The Feats of Strength.

"I need you to go trick-or-treating with me," she said.

He shook his head. He had his eyes closed, because he was reclined on the beach chair with his face directly in the sun. She found herself staring at his face in the dappled light coming through the tree. Fortunately, he couldn't see her staring with his eyes closed.

"I can't, Est. You know my mom and I have our tradition. It's the only time all week I'm going to get to see her for longer than five minutes."

Esther plopped down on the grass next to his chair, her back on a Sample gravestone. "She's been really busy, huh."

"Yeah. I get it. She wasn't raised with much money,

and this business is doing really well. It's our family's way to a better future. For me, especially. But still, it sucks not seeing her."

Esther felt terrible asking, but without Agustín, there would be no real Halloween for her this year. "There's another part to the favor."

He turned his head and opened his eyes to a suspicious narrow. She quickly looked away from his face and pretended to study the gravestones.

"What?" he said.

Agustín and his mother had a tradition. She hated the kids that liked to hang out in her front yard on Halloween and saw the whole holiday as disrespectful to the calling she took very seriously, so a few years before she had offered Agustín a deal. They would skip trick-or-treating. Skip Halloween altogether. In exchange, she would take him to a movie on Halloween night, and then the next day she would take him to the store and buy him some of the bags of heavily discounted candy. That way, he got to have fun and also have candy, and she didn't have to worry about being home on a holiday she hated. He had eagerly taken her up on that. He didn't care about Halloween either way, and as long as he also got candy, seeing a movie was as good as trick-or-treating.

Esther was baffled by that idea. She genuinely couldn't understand why anyone would agree to that. But now the arrangement could be her lifeline.

"I need to tell my parents that I'm going with you and your mom to the movies."

"But instead, you'll be trick-or-treating."

"No. Instead we'll both be trick-or-treating." She said this with the conviction she felt deep inside. She wanted to trick-or-treat, so she would, which meant Agustín would say yes because he just had to.

"Sorry, Est. I like the movies. And I hate Halloween. Trick-or-treating is your thing. It's not mine."

"Please."

He laughed.

"Man, it must be serious if it has you acting so polite. But no."

She put her hand on his arm. It was only supposed to be a way of getting his attention, but they both froze for a moment when she did it. Things had been different between them in the last year or so, although neither of them could quite say how. Where once there had been the open borders of friendship, now there seemed to be walls and pitfalls they never saw coming until they ran into them. And here was one now, the reaction they both had when she touched his arm. She took her hand back and turned away, looking at a gravestone that had a meticulously carved angel posed upon it.

"Please, Agustín. Just this year. For me."

He squinted at her as if she were a stranger he was trying to get to know, and then relaxed and closed his eyes against the late-afternoon warmth.

"Ah, my mom kept complaining about having to take time off to go out tomorrow anyway. She has a deadline soon. Kept saying it was going to put her behind. She'll probably be happy." He sighed. "She always has a deadline soon."

"Well." Esther didn't know what to say to that. "Thank you" is all she had to offer.

"What am I supposed to wear? I don't do costumes."

"My brother has some old ones. You can wear one of those."

He let out another long sigh, but he didn't seem that annoyed. It was more that he felt like he should be annoyed, and so was putting on a performance of irritation.

"You owe me, Esther Gold."

"I owe you," she agreed.

"Hey, did you see the news about that guy who got arrested near here?" he said.

They moved easily back into conversation, the negotiation done with, promises made.

"No? Why? Where?"

"Up in the hills. You know, where the big houses are. Some guy had all this stolen art and artifacts. Millions of dollars' worth of stuff taken from museums. Like, art that has been listed as missing for hundreds of years."

"Wow. How did he get caught?"

"That's what's weird. Someone robbed him, and right before they did, they called the cops. Told the cops they were going to rob him."

"Why would they do that?"

"I guess they only took one thing. By the standards of this guy's collection it was barely valuable, some exhibit stolen from a science museum's van a few years back. Cops think that maybe the robbers weren't in it to get a big haul, but only wanted to call attention to the guy. He's going to jail for a long time."

"Wow," she said.

"Right? Think about what might be going on in all these houses around us. What other secrets are there?"

He got out of the beach chair, using the gravestone next to him to haul himself up. The vines growing between the gravestones crunched under his feet.

"Better go break the news to Mom. See you tomorrow."

"Thank you, Agustín."

"Pick me out a cool costume, okay?"

She giggled, and then was embarrassed that she had done that. She walked back home, blushing about having giggled, and that made her giggle again. *Knock it off*, she told herself. But that only made her blush harder.

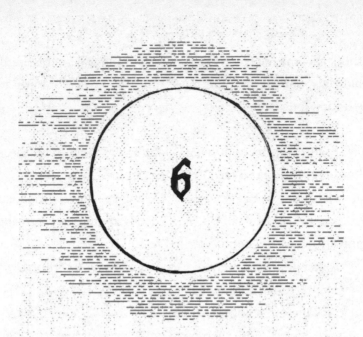

ESTHER LIKED TO WATCH scary movies while she prepared her costumes. It put her in the right mood for the occasion.

Halloween was a day in which you could pretend you were inside a horror story. Now, maybe most people wouldn't want to be inside a horror story. But as far as Esther could see it, the real world was pretty scary itself. And the real world was scary in a way that was simultaneously boring and difficult. Whereas horror stories were scary in a way that was exciting and simple and, most important, not real. They were a way to think about very scary stuff in a very safe way.

Right now she was watching a movie about a teenage girl being followed by a monster that no one understood. The movie didn't understand it. There was nothing to understand.

All that anyone needed to know was that this monster would follow the girl until it caught her, and she must never let it catch her. It was one of Esther's favorite movies.

All of this was happening in her bedroom, because she couldn't let her parents know she was preparing costumes. Still, they knew. They understood what a closed bedroom door and the sound of a horror movie meant. They pretended they didn't so there didn't need to be a big confrontation about it.

She had edited her three costumes down to two. The one she had originally planned for trick-or-treating was too obvious—a reference to a viral video that, in retrospect, was likely to inspire half the costumes on the block—and so it had to be abandoned. She had moved to her backup costume, a horror movie villain of her own invention, that, fortunately for her plan to deceive her parents, looked a lot like a person wearing normal clothes until the makeup and fake wound patches she had ordered online made it all horrifying.

The costume for school was the same as it had been from the start. The idea of it was so clever that she couldn't have abandoned it, and anyway her parents didn't care about her wearing a costume to school. One part of the costume unexpectedly popped and fizzed, and she prodded it to try to understand what was going wrong with the mechanism. It was all pretty complicated, but she had built it herself, so it didn't take her long to find the tube that had a loose seal and fix it with some duct tape. She put the entire mechanism on and pressed the button in her palm. There was the satisfying hiss of it all working perfectly.

A couple perfunctory knocks and then her dad opened her bedroom door.

"Whoa. Cool." He frowned. "That's for school, right?"

"Yes, Dad."

"Thank you, honey. I know. You hate us. But it's just . . . it's time. This is the year."

"It's fine, Dad. I'm going with Agustín to see a movie."

"Oh wow. Okay. Perfect. Hey, do you want to see something a little funny?"

He indicated toward the front window, and she followed him out. Parked down the block was another ice cream truck, playing a discordant, mournful waltz.

"Heard that song and couldn't stand it," her dad said. He was very sensitive to pitch. "But funny, right? Who sells fruit from an ice cream truck?"

This truck had a picture of a big rosy apple, like the kind that would be poisoned in a fairy tale. Every part of the truck, from the tires to the warbling speakers up top, was pristine. "Queen of Halloween Apples. They Have a Bite!" said the text under the picture of the apple.

"Should we?" her dad asked.

Esther remembered the other truck, the much dirtier one, and the sullen man driving it.

"I don't think so. It seems weird."

"Ah, it's worth a shot," her dad said. He went outside and, after a moment of hesitating, she went after.

"Hi there," her dad called as they approached the truck. "Selling apples?"

Esther couldn't see through the truck's window as they approached, and all at once she didn't want to see inside of it. She was sure there was a ghoulish creature waiting there. The moment that they came close enough, a horrifying face would appear and she would drop dead merely from the sight of it. She was as certain of this as of her own name.

But her dad was walking on, and she couldn't let him confront alone whatever waited inside the truck. She held her breath and stepped a little closer, and then the window popped open. A man stuck his head out. He was a pleasant-looking man in his twenties wearing a neat white uniform with a white paper hat. His hair was combed back under the hat. Every detail about him was exactly in the right place.

"Good evening, sir," the young man said. "I'm afraid not just yet. Tomorrow is when business starts."

"Scouting out the area?" her dad said.

The man smiled. It was wide and friendly, but also practiced. Esther felt that if the man smiled a thousand times, each one would land in exactly the same way. It had the forced, repetitive execution of a teacher trying to make "good morning" sound cheery on the third month of the school year.

"Something like that," the man said. He held out his hand. "Dan Apel."

"Dan Apple?" her dad asked, shaking the hand.

The man looked furious for a moment, a violent and animal rage, but then his placid smile was back, broad and warm, exactly where it had been. The shift was so quick that Esther wasn't sure she had seen it.

"Apel," he said. "Similar, I know. But at least I'm not my brother."

"Is he the one with the pumpkin truck?" Esther asked.

The man shifted his smile to her, like a spotlight seeking out an escaped prisoner.

"Why yes, you must have seen him driving around. I apologize for the state of his truck, he doesn't have the same enthusiasm for customer service that I do. But yes, he sells pumpkins."

"Why did you say at least you're not your brother?" she asked.

"His name is Ed Pumken. You can imagine the confusion."

"Why do you have different last names?"

He leaned down toward her. His smile was like a paper-thin mask, and she felt there was a face so terrible it hardly was human waiting right behind it.

"You ask a lot of questions," he said. Then he laughed, and he was genuine and happy again. "Well, thanks for stopping by. Hope to see you both tomorrow."

"Sure," her dad said. "This is a real interesting business idea. I'll have to keep my eye on that. I'm always interested in how people run small businesses. I run a wedding band, you see."

"I see," the man said. "Thanks for saying so." He looked

down at Esther. "I'll have my eye out for you tomorrow. See you then."

There was ice in his voice. Her dad didn't seem to hear it. He walked back toward the house, chuckling, and Esther hurried ahead of him, wanting to get as far from the truck as possible.

"What an interesting young man," her dad said.

She looked back. Dan Apel was watching them, no sign of a smile on his face.

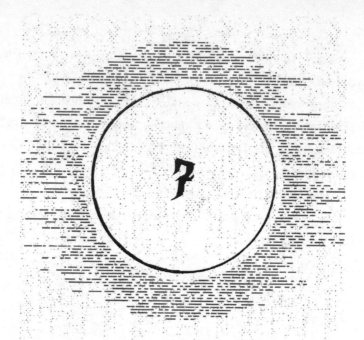

THAT NIGHT, Esther had trouble falling asleep. She always did, the night before Halloween.

She thought through her costumes, and how amazed everyone would be by them, and she started bopping her head on her pillow. Then she thought about how she had made Agustín break his tradition with his mother and how she would be tricking her parents, and she bopped her head a little less.

Was she in the wrong here? Probably. But she was human. Didn't she deserve to be in the wrong sometimes?

Next year she would be open with them about trick-or-treating. Or she wouldn't. She'd figure it out when she got there.

But enough guilt. Her bedside clock ticked over, silently, digitally, to midnight. It was officially Halloween. She forgave her own imperfections, and allowed herself to feel only excitement. Her favorite day of the year had come.

There was a hacking cough from outside her window. Then noises of an engine barely holding it together. She sat up in bed and looked out. The ice cream truck that sold pumpkins was limping its way down the street, black smoke pouring from its hood. Ed Pumken was in the driver's seat, one arm out the window. As he drove under a streetlight, she saw a glimpse of his face, as grumpy as before, and his crooked hat and uncombed hair. What was he doing driving around this late? She didn't trust him or his brother.

There was movement behind the truck. A small group of children in Halloween costumes, running in formation. Their costumes were ragged and torn. One child was dressed as an astronaut. Another as a dinosaur. A third as a wizard. But it looked like their costumes had been buried for years and then dug up. Even as they passed in and out of the streetlights, she still couldn't quite see their faces.

What she was seeing scared her. Not like how going to high school next year scared her, or not like how it scared her that Grandma Debbie went out of her house less and less and seemed to remember Esther less and less every time she saw her, and Grandma Debbie might die soon, which Esther knew was just a natural part of life but still refused to accept, unwilling to let the version of her grandmother she remembered as a child disappear into whatever was going to happen to Grandma Debbie next. Nothing as complicated as that. What she was seeing now scared her like a scary movie. It scared directly and simply. She didn't quite believe what she was seeing, even as she had no choice but to admit that she was seeing it.

A long shadow unwound itself, covering the whole of the street. The source of the shadow was out of view of her window. Ed slowed his truck to a groaning halt. He got out of the truck, wiping at his grease-stained uniform. His paper hat had fallen crumpled on the floor by the driver's seat, and his hair hung over his face. He walked slowly toward the source of the shadow, and the children in costumes followed him. Then he stopped and got down on his knees, right in the middle of the street. The children did the same.

He and the trick-or-treaters bowed, pressing their foreheads to the asphalt. What were they bowing to? Esther strained her face against the glass, trying to see, but all she managed to do was fog the window. She was afraid to move to another window. Better maybe that she not know. Better maybe that she never find out.

Ed rose back to his knees. His forehead was red where he had pushed it into the street.

"Your Highness," he said. "All is prepared." He did not sound like he was shouting, but his voice echoed eerily off the sidewalk and the houses, and Esther could easily hear every word.

The children, also back up on their knees, made a buzzing, clicking sound, like insects.

"Great," said a commanding voice from outside Esther's view. "I'll tell you what, that is absolutely fantastic. Just great work from all of you."

"Thank you, Your Highness," Ed said.

"You can go now," the voice said. "You're dismissed or whatever."

"Thank you, Your Highness."

"Stop thanking me, and put your stringy hair back in your truck and drive somewhere I can't see you."

"Yes, Your Highness." He jumped up. He no longer looked grumpy, but terrified. He jogged to the truck, glancing fearfully behind him.

"My children, with me," said the voice. "We still have so much to prepare. No rest for the wicked and all that."

More buzzing and clicking, and the trick-or-treaters ran out of sight as Ed made a laborious three-point turn and drove in the other direction.

What in the world had Esther just seen? She lay back down, wide eyes on the ceiling, and did not sleep for hours. She couldn't tell whether she was excited that this Halloween was turning out truly weird and creepy, or terrified that figures straight out of her horror movies were standing in her street. She went back and forth with herself between the two feelings all night, before finally drifting off as the sun hit her face, never having settled on an answer.

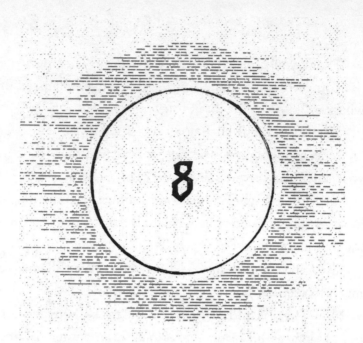

THE NEXT MORNING, everyone in the family was worried. Esther Gold, who loved Halloween more than anyone else, was not wearing a costume.

"Are you feeling okay?" her dad said, putting his hand on her forehead.

"I'm fine," she said, into her bowl of cereal.

"Is this because of what we said?" her mom asked, walking through the kitchen with coat and keys in hand, on her way to work. "Because if this is your response, you're only hurting yourself, you know."

"I'm not hurting anyone," Esther said. "No one is hurt. Everyone is fine."

Her little sister, Sharon, didn't say anything, but looked up at her with wide eyes. Esther winked at her sister, who giggled. Her sister liked winking but didn't understand what a wink meant.

"Not to take our parents' side on anything," her older brother, Ben, said, eating a breakfast bar while leaning on the counter, "but if you're not wearing a costume, I'm thinking it's the end of the world. Or like, time's about to stand still."

"Maybe it *is* the end of the world," she said.

"Ha! Cool," he said.

"Ben, knock it off," her mom said, bustling back in because she had forgotten her wallet.

"I'm just saying, like, hypothetically it would be cool."

"Cool," Sharon said. "Cool." She clapped her hands.

"Oh great," her dad said. "She's learned that word. Now she has ninety percent of the vocabulary she'll use as a teenager."

"You've never sounded more like a dad," Esther said.

"She's right," Ben said. "But that's okay. Dads are cool now."

"Knock it off, both of you," her mom said, then stopped and sat at the table. "I forgot to eat breakfast. I should eat breakfast."

"Esther, honey, it's Halloween," her dad said. "I've never seen you anything but giddy on Halloween. What happened?"

Had something happened? That depended on what she had seen. But she had no idea what she had seen. She didn't know if it was real. And if it was real, she didn't know what it meant. And without knowing what it meant, it was hard to think anything about it at all.

But certainly it pulled at her. It definitely brought the holiday mood of the morning down.

"I've got to go to school," she said.

"I'll drive you," her mom said.

"Mom, you never drive me. I can walk."

"I'll drive you on the way to work. Come on." Her mom, still having not eaten breakfast, grabbed her things and headed out the door.

"You sure you don't want to change into your costume before going?" her dad asked. "It looked pretty cool when you were trying it on last night. Hate to let an idea that cool go to waste."

"You just said cool twice in ten seconds. Who has the limited vocabulary now?" Ben said, throwing away the breakfast bar wrapper and grabbing his backpack as his friend Kyle pulled up out front.

"No, that's okay, Dad," Esther said, ignoring her brother. "I'm okay."

Her dad watched his older kids scatter out on their way to school, and then he turned back to Sharon.

"Well, at least you're not insulting me yet," he said.

Sharon threw a slice of apple at him and clapped again.

Her mom was waiting outside, but the car wasn't on.

"Come on," her mom said. "You're right. The school's nearby. We'll walk."

"But you have to get to work."

"I'm always so early, I have time to walk you to school before I go."

This was the last year Esther would be making this trip by foot. Next year was high school, too far to walk. She would have to be driven, or bike there. The bike ride went along a busy road, not like this peaceful stretch of suburban streets.

And high school itself was a blank, a mystery. No matter what Ben or her parents said to her about it, she couldn't picture what it would be like for her. She felt the mystery in her gut. It felt like seeing whatever ritual had happened out on the street last night. That feeling of witnessing something that she should never have seen, of entering a dark world she had no interest in entering.

"I wanted to have some time with you this morning," her mom said, "because you've definitely been acting strangely since our talk yesterday. But instead of you shouting and me grounding you, I thought we could try to just talk about it. Understand each other."

"That's very adult of you," Esther said.

"Funny, kid."

"Funny kid," she agreed, indicating herself.

Aware of how few times she had left to do this walk before she changed to the high school across town, she really tried to hold on to every detail of it. The prickly juniper bushes along the sidewalk. The dry eastern wind, blowing the clouds the wrong way across the sky. The orange groves on the hill above the housing development. In season, the trees burst orange with ripening fruit, a Southern California version of autumn.

"Someday they'll probably cut those orchards down," Esther's mom said. "Build houses over them. They've done it everywhere else."

"I choose to believe those trees will never go," Esther said. "The hills will be orange and green forever."

"Forever is quite a word."

"I used to think this walk took forever," Esther said. "Like it never seemed to end. Now it feels like it's going so fast. I want this walk to be so much longer."

"Time keeps happening for all of us," her mom said. "I know you love Halloween, but I don't think this is about trick-or-treating. You knew you'd have to stop doing that eventually. We had talked about it. I think this might just be about . . . I don't know. You're growing up, Esther."

"I'm only thirteen," she said.

"And I'm only forty-three." Her mom smiled. "I know that sounds ancient, it did to me once, but not anymore. We're all only the age we are until we're the next age after that. If we're lucky."

"This is quite a pep talk."

"I'm not here to cheer you up, Esther. Your dad can do that. Play some saxophone for you or something. I'm here to say that you turn fourteen soon, and you'll be going to high school, and you'll be a teenager, and I imagine that's scary. It's scary for me."

Esther thought about how much of the truth to reveal. The sky was so blue that it seemed translucent, like she could see the dark of space through the thin edges of it. Already, even at this hour of the morning, it was warm. Every time the wind blew, there was the smell of dust and plants and herbs, a smell that for the rest of her life would belong to her childhood.

"Yeah, it's really scary," she admitted finally.

"Yeah," her mom agreed.

"Well, what should I do about it? You're the parent. You're supposed to have advice."

"Oh man, I *am* the parent, aren't I?" Her mom laughed. "I don't know, baby. It's scary. I guess that's my first advice. Growing up never stops being scary. But it'll happen either way."

"Just toughen up and live with it?" Esther said. "That's what you've got for me?"

"It can be exciting, growing up. The future can be scary, but it can be thrilling too. Change can be good. I guess that's my parental advice. That's the best I've got."

"Thanks, Mom. It was very wise and all that."

"Smart mouth." They both laughed.

A black cat darted out of the bushes and tore across the sidewalk. Esther screamed a little in surprise.

"Ew, bad luck on Halloween," Esther said, recoiling.

"You know," her mom said, "that's a dangerous myth. Black cats are just cats. Living creatures like you. But they get hurt and killed by ignorant people because of a stupid story that they're bad luck. We should work to be better than that. Treat living creatures as worth our respect, no matter what silly stories we've been told about them."

Esther watched the cat run down the street.

"Huh. Sorry, little kitten," she called after it.

The cat disappeared back into the shadows of someone's front yard.

"I won't make you walk with me all the way to the school

gate," her mom said. "Don't want to embarrass you. Just wanted some time together."

"Thanks, Mom." They hugged, and her mom kissed her cheek.

"So can I go trick-or-treating one last time this year?"

"No."

"Worth a shot."

"Goodbye, Esther Gold."

Esther walked the last few blocks to school, really trying to experience and remember each step. Up on the hills, leaves rustled in the orange trees, soaking up a sun so warm and gentle it felt like it would never stop shining.

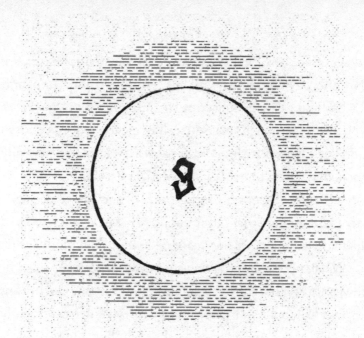

THE CROWD GOING INTO school was packed with aliens and superheroes and video game characters. Every grade higher had fewer costumes than the one below. Among the eighth graders, only about half dressed up. But still, there would be a parade for them too, and a best costume would be picked.

Esther had won her grade's contest every year, except the year that Brad Winters had dressed up as the hero from the big movie of that summer using an actual prop from the movie that his dad had bought at an auction. Everyone had been so impressed that part of his costume had touched a famous person, and so the title had been stolen from her. She had never quite forgiven Brad for that.

Brad had tried the same trick the next year, but his dad could only afford a prop from a movie that hadn't done well at the box office and that no one in school had seen. No one was impressed with his leftovers from a flop, and Esther had easily beaten him by dressing up as New York City, different neighborhoods all over her arms and torso and legs, and a little yellow cab on tracks that actually moved between them. It had been almost impossible to sit down, and kids kept breaking parts of the city off by accident and on purpose, but it had totally been worth it. Brad hadn't tried to match her again.

When people saw her wearing ordinary clothes on Halloween, they stared. Everyone knew what this day meant to Esther Gold. And even though they didn't care nearly as much about the holiday as she did, they all looked forward to what she would come up with. The idea that she wouldn't come up with anything had never occurred to them, and even the teachers felt a pang of disappointment.

"What's the matter, Esther Gold?" Sasha Min said, blocking her way. "Too cheap to spend money on a costume this year?"

This was about Esther being Jewish. It wasn't a big deal, but also it was. It was both at once.

The thing of it was that no one in school actively hated Jews, not that she knew of. But there was a blindness there, an erasure. She was the only one, and so there was this sense that perhaps she was only pretending, that no one else in the world was Jewish and Esther had invented it all just to inconvenience them.

She especially hated the money jokes. There was a time

in Europe in which Jews had been banned from almost every job, among other indignities and violence. The few jobs available to them were peddling and moneylending. These were not occupations they sought out, but the ones that were left for them, like scraps. And then, when they did those jobs, because they were human beings who needed to survive, the world punished them for it. Branding them as cheap because peddlers need to haggle, branding them as greedy because moneylenders work with debts. Like many stories of a minority group, it is the story of people being forced into a corner and then stereotyped for the corner they had been forced into.

All of this went through her head very quickly. Other things were probably going through Sasha's head. Esther supposed that we all go through life with a whole lot of ourselves between us and the world.

"That's not funny, Sasha," she said.

"I think it's funny. I think it's funny that you're too cheap to buy a costume even though that's the only thing you care about. I think that's the funniest thing in the world."

No one knew why Sasha and Esther hated each other. Even they didn't know. Sure, it hadn't started well in third grade, when Sasha had earnestly explained to Esther that she had learned about Jewish people at church and the Jews were the ones who had murdered Jesus. It wasn't meant as an insult, just a child helpfully sharing a fact she had been taught.

"You guys murdered Jesus," she'd said to Esther. "Why did you do that?"

"We didn't."

"Well, you did."

What had started as a child's misunderstanding turned into an argument and then into a feud, and then Sasha had started seeking her out, bullying her at every opportunity.

Sasha no longer believed that the Jews killed Jesus. She didn't even dislike Jewish people. At this point, she just disliked Esther Gold, and she used whatever tools she could find at hand to hurt her. Sometimes, at home, she would think about what she had said and feel guilty, and the guilt would hollow a sharp pain inside her chest. But the next day she would say something again. As the skinny daughter of Korean immigrants, she had learned early that bullying was a fact of school, and that it would always be better to be the bully than the bullied. It was the same reason she was the most aggressive player on her soccer team, sweeping people off their feet with her long legs.

No matter how much she bullied Esther, it didn't keep the other kids from making jokes about Sasha's family, and the way that Sasha looked. Esther felt bad for her in those moments when Sasha would blush and tremble with an anger that Esther recognized in herself. There was so much anger about what they were each experiencing, and so little that was useful to do with that anger. The two of them were caught in something heavy and tangled and vast, and neither of them could see a way out.

This Halloween morning, Sasha got right in Esther's face. Kids gathered around the two of them. Teachers came hurrying over to stop whatever was happening before it got too far.

Esther smiled at Sasha. She pressed a button in her palm. There was a hiss from the air compressor in her backpack, and that's when the two other heads inflated from her shoulders with a loud pop. Hideous faces, leering and sudden. Sasha screamed and fell over backward.

"Oh, I am wearing a costume, actually," Esther said. "But thanks for your concern."

"Esther Gold, leave Sasha alone," Mr. Reynolds, the sixth-grade math teacher, said absently, never looking up from his phone.

Agustín came up next to her.

"That's maybe the best one yet," he said.

"Right?" she said. She pressed the button again, and the heads started to deflate back into their hiding places. The noise was, well, a little farty. People laughed. Even Mr. Reynolds smirked. Plus the heads didn't quite go back in neatly and she had to awkwardly shove them into their pouches on her shoulder blades.

"Alright, they still have a few issues I'm working out," she said.

Sasha was helped up by her friends and glared at Esther, but seemed to be done saying anything.

"Did you tell your mom?" Esther asked Agustín.

He rolled his eyes. "Yeah, she pretended to be annoyed, but I think secretly she was glad. She'll be in her workshop all night, won't even notice I'm not there."

"I'm sure she wanted to go with you," Esther tried.

"Come on," Agustín said. "We'll be late."

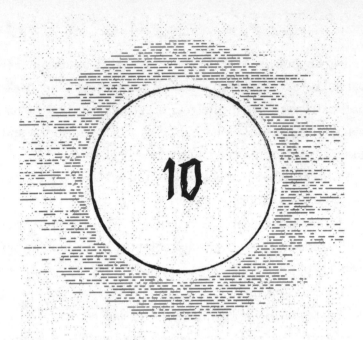

10

SCHOOL WENT ON normally from there. Throughout the day, kids (and a few teachers) would come to her asking to see the trick with the heads. And, with a pop, two new heads would sprout from her shoulders. She learned to accept their amazement and then quietly maneuver herself somewhere private for the less dignified act of resetting the whole contraption.

Sasha Min watched her from across the outdoor lunch tables, whispering darkly to her friends. This being Southern California, there was no cafeteria, nor were there really hallways. Anything that could be outside, was outside. On the few days a year it rained, they would have lunch in the classrooms as the miserable teachers missed their breaks to monitor them. But mostly they ate outside, played outside, and went between classes outside.

The yard of the school was broad, a huge expanse of lawn, five acres or more, now crowded with costumed students parading. Esther won her grade, of course. She waited until halfway through the parade to activate the extra heads, and even the many kids who had seen them before applauded. It was a really good effect. She didn't win every year out of legacy. She worked for and earned every win. She was great at Halloween.

Brad Winters was dressed in a store-bought zombie costume. He had given up trying.

As Esther accepted the prize, a brief ceremony that was important only to her, she looked over the crowd of kids who were no longer paying attention and had moved on to shoving each other and playing basketball in full costume. Esther saw something that made her heart beat strangely.

It was a woman, standing in the park on the other side of the fence from the school. She was wearing an old-style gown, Victorian maybe, although Esther had never been particularly good with fashion. Clothes only interested her when they were called costumes.

This didn't look like a costume. This didn't look like a woman dressed up as a Victorian lady for Halloween. The woman looked like she lived in those clothes, and she looked as lost in time as her dress. Her hair was piled on itself, messy but in a way that seemed intentional, and her face was the imperious face of a woman used to giving orders and having those orders followed. Or else.

The woman was watching the Halloween parade from

the edge of the canyon. *The bottom of her dress must be getting filthy in the dust*, Esther thought. It was when she thought this that she realized what else was peculiar about what she was seeing.

The woman's feet were not touching the ground. She was floating several inches off the dirt.

"Take the award, Esther. Come on, stop dragging this out," Mrs. Hooper said, thrusting it at her again. Esther took the piece of paper, hot from the break room printer, and said, "Thanks, Mrs. Hooper."

She looked back to the canyon, but the woman was gone. *No one floats.* Esther wasn't the best in science class, but she understood that no one floats. What she had seen wasn't real. But she had seen it. The woman's face had been set into a cruel sneer, like she had done terrible things and planned to do even more terrible things soon. It was impossible that she had seen the woman. She knew she had seen the woman.

"If even Esther doesn't care," said Mrs. Hooper, "then I don't know why we do this whole prize thing." She grumbled the whole way back to the office. "How did Howard convince me to be in charge of this anyway? I don't even like Halloween."

11

SCHOOL ENDED, and the flood of imaginary characters, shorter and younger than traditionally portrayed, roared out the front gates. There was excited talk of who was going to what party or going trick-or-treating where.

No one should have been more excited than Esther, but she felt weighed down by the odd things she had seen. The creepy apple man and those weird kids last night were one thing, but what to say about a woman whose feet did not touch the ground?

Agustín could tell she was bothered, but he misunderstood the source of it.

"Man, I know, I know," he said. He did not know. "It sucks that your parents are making you sneak around like this, but you're smart. You'll get away with it."

"Thanks to you."

"That's right," he said, laughing. "Don't forget it either."

"See you later?"

"My mom will be back in her workshop all afternoon. It's been really busy lately. Which is good, I guess. But mind if I walk with you for a bit?"

"What is it this time?"

"What is it any time? I mean, she makes money. Got us our house in this bougie white neighborhood. So. But it'd be nice to see her more." He tried to play it off as complaining, but his voice was deeply and truly sad. "Just be nice to see her more is all."

As they walked down the sidewalk, Sasha Min's mom leaned out of her minivan.

"Hey, kids, sure I can't drive you home?"

"No, Mom!" Sasha said from the passenger seat.

"Sasha Elizabeth Min, you will be polite or you will be walking home," her mom snapped. This was an empty threat, as there was no way that she would ever let Sasha walk home.

Esther found herself feeling sorry for Sasha, who had never wandered the after-school sidewalks, the neighborhood yards, or the dirt trails in the canyon. So much of Esther's life was made of those wanderings, and it seemed that so much of Sasha's was from the passenger seat of that car. Then she caught herself. What did she care about Sasha's life?

"That's okay, Mrs. Min," Esther said. "I like walking."

"How about you, Agustín?" Mrs. Min said.

Sasha stared glumly at her feet.

"No, Mrs. Min. That's very nice of you," he said. "We're going to walk."

Sasha's mom shook her head, clearly baffled by the choices that some people make.

"If you're sure," she said, and turned on the engine.

"Thank god," Sasha said, loudly and clearly.

"Sasha, you knock it off right now or I won't take you trick-or-treating."

Esther and Agustín walked away laughing.

"Looks like someone is in trouble," he said.

They crossed the park next to the school. She couldn't stop staring at the place where the woman had been. Now it was only another part of the park. A man was throwing tennis balls for three pit bulls who scrambled and wrestled on their way to fetching them. The high school cross-country team was running on a long loop back to the school. A group of community college students were parked in the lot, hanging out and eating fast food. Everything was normal. She had mistaken what she had seen was all. Still, she couldn't make herself believe that.

"Gus, you should go to the movies with your mom."

He glared at her. "You're changing your mind now? I already canceled on her."

"No, not changing my mind, no. It's just . . ." She tried to find a way to form the thought that wouldn't offend him or make him feel pitied. Feeling pitied was horrible. "It's just you haven't gotten to see your mom much lately. Because of how busy she is. I mean, you see me every day. So I appreciate what you're doing, but maybe you should spend that time with your mom, not me."

He stopped walking, so she stopped walking.

"Est, listen. She makes the choices she makes. You didn't make those choices for her. If my mom wanted to see me more, she could see me more. You're not responsible for that. Don't try to fix my relationship with my mom, okay?"

He turned and started walking again, faster than before. She hurried to catch up.

"Okay, sorry, I just thought—"

"You were wrong. How's the essay in English going for you?"

She accepted this change of subject gratefully, a sign that he had no interest in spending the day annoyed with her. "Mostly good. Geometry though, right?"

He stuck his tongue out at her. "I'm doing pretty great in geometry actually."

They made their way down into the canyon. With Agustín at her side, the tunnel didn't creep her out. Instead, it was merely a nice respite from the sun. As pleasant as the weather in Southern California was, sometimes all any of them wanted was an escape from it. Thus the hours spent inside on the internet, looking at pictures of the world outside, or under the blue chemical waters of swimming pools, smelling chlorine instead of sagebrush.

"Feats of Strength," she blurted.

"What, really?"

They hadn't done a game of Feats of Strength in a year, partly because they felt like maybe they had outgrown it, and partly because their parents would kill them if they found out.

But Esther was already clambering up the rocks on the side of the tunnel entrance, so Agustín took after her. They scooted carefully over the narrow ledge and then back down the rocks on the other side.

Then into the drainpipe. She had grown a bit since the last time they had done this, and it was even tighter than she remembered, squeezing at her shoulders. She didn't want to think what would happen if she got stuck. The worst part was when the pipe turned, and everything was completely dark for several feet until you felt the exit to your left, and made your way down the even more narrow pipe to the bit of sunlight ahead, hoping no snakes had decided to make their home in the darkness. She pushed her way out and ran up the hill, dodging cacti.

Agustín's shoulders had gotten broader, and so he struggled to get out of the drainpipe, but he finally was up the hill too. Then along the top of the hill, to the final ledge, where Esther was waiting, looking down at the pond far below.

"This time I'm gonna do it," she said.

"Man, don't do that," he said. "That water is disgusting."

And the fall is so far, she could feel him thinking, because she was thinking it too.

"If we don't do it now," she said, "when are we going to

do it? We're getting too old for this game."

He took her point, but it didn't make the ledge they were on any less high.

"Do you really want to explain to your mom why you're soaked through with gutter water?" he said. "Because I don't."

"Alright," she said. "Another Feats of Strength without a winner. Except I won."

"No one won."

"I got to the end first."

"It doesn't count if you didn't actually finish."

They argued happily down to the trail and up the steep slope out of the canyon, back up to the streets. Mr. Nathaniel was out washing his car, of course. When he saw them, he stopped the spray of the water.

"Hey, kids," he barked.

Esther couldn't remember a time he had ever talked to any of them. His voice was higher and lighter than she expected, given his age and his constant glower. They kept walking, unsure of how to ignore him but desperately wanting to.

"Hey, kids," he said again. They stopped.

"Do you smell that?" Mr. Nathaniel said.

"What?" Agustín said.

Mr. Nathaniel took a long sniff in. They could hear the mucus in his nasal passages and were both silently grossed out, but there was something magnetic about how unabashed he was. When he was done with his snorting, he shook his head.

"Unmistakable, that smell." He pointed at them, a finger

that was halfway between cautionary and accusing. "You kids stay inside this evening. Stay safe. It's a Halloween moon tonight."

"Okay, Mr. Nathaniel," Esther said.

One more loud sniff, then Mr. Nathaniel went back to spraying his car.

"Unmistakable. She'll be out tonight," he muttered.

The two of them took the opportunity to speed-walk away.

"What a psycho," Agustín said. "I'm glad I'm not his neighbor."

"Thanks," she said.

Mr. Gabler was pulling into his drive. "Oh, hi there, Esther," he said as he got out of his car.

"Hello, Mr. Gabler," she said. "Home early?"

He grinned. "Not a lot of dental appointments on Halloween afternoon for some reason. See you tonight?"

He held up the plastic shopping bag full of miniature tubes of toothpaste.

"Maybe!" she said, as brightly as she could in order to hide her disgust.

"I know, I know, not as exciting as candy, but you can get candy anywhere else. You can only get dental health from one place. Say hi to your folks for me."

He cheerily carried the plastic bags of toothpaste that no child would ever use into the house.

As Esther and Agustín neared her corner, they slowed down.

"See you in a couple hours?" he said.

"Yeah," she said. "I'll bring a costume for you." She looked thoughtfully back the way they had come. "He's not wrong, you know."

"That Mr. Gabler's house is the only place you can get dental health?"

"No, what Mr. Nathaniel said. Tonight will be the first Halloween full moon in nineteen years."

"So you think we should stay inside for our safety?"

"Are you kidding? I would hate to miss the only time I'll ever be able to go trick-or-treating under a full moon. It's going to be so cool."

"Alright, Halloween Girl, see you then." He started toward his house.

She stayed on her front steps for a bit, trying to get as excited about tonight as she wanted to be. As she stood there, she heard what sounded like the laughter of children, but with a grating, mechanical edge to it. She looked up to see, at the end of the block, a small group of trick-or-treaters. A clown. A robot. And a dinosaur. Dirty. Costumes ripped. Faces turned so she couldn't see what they looked like. The kids were running after someone who had already passed out of sight around the corner. Esther could just see the adult's long shadow in the afternoon sunlight, and then the shadow was gone, and then the children were gone too.

"Happy Halloween," she said to herself. "Looks like it's going to be a scary one."

THE AFTERNOON PASSED in a blur of nervousness and homework. She had never snuck out like this on her parents. But she didn't have any choice. They were keeping her from her most important holiday. It was like persecution or something.

Once her homework was done, she put on another of her favorite scary movies. This was about a rich family in an isolated house deep in the woods. Men with animal masks start attacking them. It was a gory movie, and Esther had to keep reminding herself how movie effects worked and that no one was actually being injured. Her parents would have shut that down pretty quick, so she kept the volume so low she could barely hear the masked men saying creepy things to each other.

Her dad practiced saxophone in the garage for hours.

She had to admit he was getting better, but woodwinds still eluded him, and he mostly sounded like someone whose lunch had disagreed with him. When she couldn't concentrate on the movie over the groaning and farting saxophone, she settled on organizing her costume and makeup. She carefully packed it all into a three-ring binder. That way she could leave home with it under the guise of taking some homework over to Agustín's house.

She knocked on her brother's door. No answer. She knocked again and then opened it a crack.

"Ben?"

But he was out with his friends, she knew he was. She also knew where he kept his old costumes, in a plastic bin on the floor of his closet, along with old T-shirts that he liked but that were too ripped up or faded to wear.

She had to wade through the sea of dirty clothes, food wrappers, and crumpled-up paper that made up the base of any teenage boy's room.

"Gross," she said, but she didn't really care. She was on a mission. She managed to open the closet door through the debris blocking it, dug around a bit, and pulled out the plastic bin of old costumes. She went through them for one that she thought Agustín wouldn't hate. Then she did her best to arrange the mess back the way it had been. She couldn't imagine her brother would have noticed if she had driven a bulldozer through his room, so she wasn't too worried about exactly how things looked when she was done. She put the folded-up costume in the now bulging binder.

As she got up to leave, she saw Sharon at the door watching her. Esther gave her another big wink. Sharon laughed and blinked back, having not yet learned how to wink herself.

Finally it was time to go meet Agustín.

"Where's Dad?" she asked her mom, who was reading the news on her phone, shoes off, feet up on the coffee table.

"He's taking a nap. Guess all that saxophone tired him out. Let's hope he sleeps through me destroying it."

Esther laughed and her mom smiled. It was a little disappointing though. Her dad was usually easier to run stuff by. He asked fewer questions.

"I'm going to head out to meet up with Agustín and his mom."

Her mom put her phone down and looked Esther in her eyes for a long moment, until Esther started to feel uncomfortable.

"Okay, hun. What movie are you seeing?"

"Um." She hadn't actually thought to look up a specific movie. The only ones she kept track of were the latest low-budget, trashy horror movies, of which there were usually a bunch around Halloween. She could rattle off a number of those that she wanted to see, but there was no chance that Agustín or his mom would have been interested in watching them, and it wouldn't have been believable at all. She realized that she could not name a single other movie that was out at the time. Well, there went the plan. It was a good try. She'd be staying in tonight after all.

"Uh," she said, "Agustín's mom isn't sure what she wants

to see. She's going to pick one when we get there."

Her mom held her gaze for a moment longer, but then she yawned deeply.

"Geez. I guess I'm more worn out than I thought. I'll probably go to bed early tonight." She shrugged, looking unable to focus on anything but how exhausting her day had been. "Okay, well have fun. Try not to wake us up when you get home."

"I won't, Mom, thank you, love you." She hugged her mom.

"Alright, alright," her mom said. "I'm probably letting you get away with something, but I'm too tired to care. It's your lucky day."

"Of course it's my lucky day," Esther said. "It's Halloween." She skipped away, threw on her costume, and grabbed the binder that the makeup was hidden in. By the time she headed out the door, her mom was already dozing off on the couch.

Esther figured that when she was older she would be that tired at the end of the day. But for now, she felt the excitement and energy of the holiday burbling inside her.

"It's Halloween!" she allowed herself to shout, scaring a dog across the street who barked grumpily at her and then went back to sleep. "It's Halloween," she said again, quieter, but no less happy.

13

"LET'S SEE IT," AGUSTÍN SAID.

She opened up the binder and pulled out the costume. It was a lime-green Star Trek uniform, a jumpsuit complete with the logo badge on the chest.

"You've got to be kidding me." But he looked kind of excited. He liked sci-fi movies.

"I would never kid you. I have no sense of humor."

"You owe me such a favor, Esther Gold."

He hurried off to try on the costume.

"Sure, sure," she called after him. "I owe you a favor. I think you owe me a favor for letting you wear that cool costume." She looked around. "Where's your mom?"

"Oh, she's already back in her workshop," Agustín shouted from the bathroom. "Left cash for dinner on the counter. She won't be out of there until real late. I get it. She's behind on a large order, and what she does is important." It didn't sound like he got it at all.

Agustín came out of the bathroom, posing in the lime-green jumpsuit. "So?" he said. Esther covered her mouth, and her entire body shook. "Stop laughing. Stop it, or you'll be going out alone tonight." He tugged at the uniform. It was a little too big for him and rode up on one side. She waved her arms in front of her, trying to find the air to say words.

"No, it's perfect. It's perfect. I'm sorry, it just took me by surprise."

"Whatever," he said. He looked at himself in the hall mirror for a long time. "I'm only doing this for you."

"And it's great. You look great. It's great."

He narrowed his eyes.

"Really!" she said. "It's fine. Let me get ready." She went in the bathroom and dumped out all the various bags of makeup, then arranged them in the order she would need them. Lots of shades of red and black and green, fake wounds, scars. She carefully applied it all to horrifying effect.

Outside she could hear him posing and jumping around in front of the mirror, sometimes even making laser sounds with his mouth. She found it cute, and then shuddered that she had thought that word about what *anyone* was doing, let alone Gus. But she did. And so even after she had applied the face of a horror movie villain over her own, she waited, letting him have a few more moments of unselfconscious joy.

Finally she got impatient and stepped out, grinning under her ghoulish makeup.

"Ah!" he said when he saw her, and not just because he had been standing with his arms on his hips, pretending that he had given the command to send an away team down to a hostile planet. "That's terrifying."

"What do you think? Did I top last Halloween?"

He looked at her carefully.

"I mean, it's scary. But . . ."

"But what?"

"Well, it's just some makeup and fake cuts and stuff."

"It took me forever to design all this!"

"Yeah, but it's no Star Trek uniform." He laughed and punched her arm lightly.

She punched back harder.

"Ow!"

"Don't trash my costume, or I'll take pictures of you wearing that and send it to everyone in school."

"You better not do that. They'll all start wanting me. There will be fights."

"See, you like Halloween."

He shook his head. "I really don't. I know you like it so much that you don't believe me. But it's okay. I'm having fun because you're having fun."

She didn't know what to say to that, so she took out a bag for her candy and thrust one at him. Outside, a couple teenagers were gathering by the gravestones in the front yard, taking selfies and laughing. Esther and Agustín would have to leave by the back to avoid getting hassled for being from the weird gravestone house. She felt sorry for him, and then felt bad about feeling sorry. He could handle himself.

"Okay there, Captain," she said.

"Okay there, Killer."

"Let's go trick-or-treating."

She felt so grateful to be saying those words. The costumes, the empty bags waiting to be filled, the neighborhood decked out in scary decorations and offering sweets to passersby. This was the best feeling in the world. Why would she ever want to grow older and leave it behind?

14

THE MOON WAS already up when they left Agustín's house. It was full and broad and candy orange against the horizon. A perfect Halloween moon.

They started their rounds on Butterfield. The folks on Butterfield put a lot of effort into their Halloween, which Esther appreciated. Mr. Winchell especially turned every inch of his yard into a Halloween display. Fake cobwebs spread over everything with the absolute Southern California confidence that it would not rain. Plastic graves and plastic zombie hands thrusting out of the dirt. Even a little maze made out of plywood that led to the front door, and a playlist of horror movie themes blaring from outdoor speakers. Esther loved it. Here was someone who cared as much as she did.

The only street that was better was Spindrift, where

there was a couple that every year turned their entire backyard into a haunted house. Nothing professional, just parents in rubber masks jumping out and waving their arms, but it showed a commitment to the spirit of the night. Esther always saved that house for last. Starting with the second-best street and ending with the best. Everything was thought through.

She felt utterly giddy as she and Agustín went up to the first house and knocked on the door. She had wanted to go trick-or-treating, and now here she was. It had all worked out. There was, she decided, no drawback to being pushy to get her way. After all, doing so had gotten her exactly what she had wanted.

"Trick or treat!" the two of them called.

The woman who answered the door, uncostumed except for a witch's hat, gave them a squinting look over.

"Bit old, aren't you?"

But she gave them candy. The next few houses didn't even make a comment, except one broad-chested, mustachioed man who pointed at Agustín's costume and said, "Hey, I love Star Wars."

Agustín wasn't sure what to say to that. "Me too?" he tried.

"Right on!" the man said, dropping candy bars into their bags. Esther and Agustín looked at each other. Once the man shut his front door they started laughing. They laughed their way back to the street.

"See," she said. "This is fun, right?"

"Yeah. But also, that lady wasn't wrong. We're a bit old."

"So we'll stop next year. Or the year after."

"Or the year after that. Yeah, you've said. I just feel silly when I never liked doing this, not even when I was little."

Esther saw that the door was open back at the first house, with the woman in the witch's hat. A small child in a pirate's costume was walking away from it. It was one of the children she had seen last night. His costume was filthy and torn. He turned toward her, as though he could feel her watching. She couldn't see his face. Where his face should have been was like a smudged photograph. Well, it was evening, and she was half a block away. It was normal to not be able to see clearly at this distance. That was probably all it was.

She turned back to Agustín, slightly ridiculous in his baggy Star Trek uniform. He was looking at her expectantly. How many days and nights had they hung out in their lives? Hundreds? And yet there were things about Agustín and her that she was just starting to notice. For instance, that his eyes were different shades of brown at different times of day. And also that she was standing here staring at his eyes, something she had never done before.

"Well," she said, "we're not going to stop this year. Anyway, the next house is my favorite. You're going to love this guy."

The next house was Mr. Winchell's house, the one that went all out every year for Halloween. Not even the most elaborate Christmas display in town could match what he did in October. Mr. Winchell was an engineer, and he put both his understanding of structure and his frustrated creative impulses into his front yard.

The looping piano of a John Carpenter soundtrack was coming from the plywood labyrinth that led to the porch. Green-faced ghouls leered from bushes and perched on the rooftops. Mr. Winchell had put a semi-transparent cloth in front of a spinning wheel of shapes he had constructed. In the light behind the cloth, the shapes became elongated shadows (witches on broomsticks, black cats arching their backs, dancing skeletons). It was a neat effect, and Esther made a mental note for when she was a grown-up and making her own lavish front yard Halloween display. She would leave out the cat, though. Black cats got a bad rap.

"Mr. Winchell is who I want to be when I grow up," she said. "Once I really am too old for trick-or-treating, I can always do this. It's almost as good."

"Guy likes playing with toys," said Agustín. She punched him again. "What? Not saying it's a bad thing. I'm dressed up like a space captain, so I'm not going to knock him for it, just making an observation."

"Observe this," she said, holding up her hand with a gesture that made Agustín laugh, and then ducking into the plywood maze as a familiar two-note string melody from a really old movie about a shark played.

Once through the maze, she was greeted by a skull over the door that maniacally laughed when its motion sensor was triggered.

"Hahahahaha," said the skull.

"Happy Halloween to you," she said.

"Hahahahaha," said the skull again, as Agustín stepped out of the maze.

Esther knocked. The moment after she did, she had an idea, and pulled Agustín behind the support pillar of the porch.

"Whoa, what are you doing?"

"We'll jump out and scare him. Boo, you know? Mr. Winchell knows me. He'll think it's funny."

"Not as funny as that skull finds everything," he said, waving his hand out from behind the pillar and getting another laugh from above the door.

"Knock it off, you'll ruin the surprise."

They waited in silence after that. A minute went by. Or maybe less than that, but squeezed behind a pillar with her friend, the wait felt endless. She noticed that Agustín no longer smelled like that mango body wash he had used for years. Now he was using something that smelled sour and chemical, a smell like gasoline and like restaurants with dress codes. The change in smell made him seem like a different person, even though in most ways he was exactly the same person. They had been friends forever. Also they had been waiting behind this pillar forever. What was taking Mr. Winchell so long?

"Hold on," she said, and knocked on the door again, darting back behind the pillar.

"This is the slowest surprise I've ever been part of," Agustín said.

They waited. Still nothing. She felt a tickling in her gut.

She didn't like the tickle, it felt wrong. She didn't want there to be something wrong, not on Halloween.

Now they both came out from behind the pillar. She knocked a third time, shouting, "Mr. Winchell?" No answer.

"Maybe he's in the bathroom."

"Gross," she said. "Shut up." But maybe. That would make sense. It would also mean that nothing was wrong, that they had just happened to come by at the wrong time.

"Alright, we'll try again later," she said. "Let's go."

She was glad there was something like an explanation, and something like a plan, but also looking back at the joyous display on Mr. Winchell's lawn, she felt nervous. All of this motion and creative expression, but the human at the heart of it was gone. Where was Mr. Winchell?

HAVING DONE ONE SIDE OF THE STREET, they crossed over and doubled back on the other. When they got to the end of that, they would swing around the corner and hit Spyglass Way, the first of the many little cul-de-sacs. It was all planned for absolute efficiency in candy collection, which Esther would then eat very little of. The candy wasn't the point. The knocking and the collecting were all that mattered to her.

But it wasn't going well. Doors went unanswered. Doors that should have been answered. Houses with porchlights on, jack-o'-lanterns set out. Fewer and fewer other kids out on the street. On their third house in a row with no answer, Agustín shook his head.

"We're trying to trick-or-treat during everyone's dinner break. This must just be exactly the wrong time."

"Gus, there's no wrong time. It's Halloween night. People don't take breaks from Halloween."

Above them, the moon was perfect and orange and huge. Merely looking at it made Esther imagine grotesque and fearsome creatures frolicking underneath it, and she shivered with happiness. But she would be happier when people started to answer their doors.

Finally, on the fourth house, someone did. The woman yawned as she opened the door, and held the yawn, nodding, as they shouted, "Trick or treat!"

"Yeah, sorry," she said, handing them each small handfuls of candy. "I've gotten so sleepy. You'll probably be my last before I go to bed. You kids be safe, okay?"

"Okay," Agustín said.

"Why is everyone so tired?" Esther said on their way back to the street. "Is this what we're going to be like when we're grown-ups? Always sleepy every night?"

"Grown-ups do get sleepy a lot, right? I feel like they're always yawning."

"I'm not looking forward to that," she said.

"Nah, me neither."

None of the doors they tried after that were answered.

"What is happening?" she said. "There's something wrong."

"People just don't care as much about Halloween as you do."

"I don't need them to care as much. I only need them to care a bit."

They got to the end of the block and turned the corner. On the other side of the street was the canyon. Even in the full moon's light, its darkness was nearly complete. Only the peaks of the hills were visible, descending quickly into the shadows of the paths. Esther shuddered a bit.

"Man, you watch too many scary movies," Agustín said. "It's the same place it was before. Just dark."

"I do watch too many scary movies. But also, come on, darkness changes a thing. The world is not just the world. The world is a story we all tell together about the world. And that story changes at night."

"Whoa. Alright there. I know you take Halloween seriously, but whoa."

"Sorry," she said. She wasn't sorry but somehow felt like she had to say it to him, although she wouldn't have been able to explain why.

The canyon wasn't entirely dark. There was a fire tucked between two of the hills. Teenagers, partying in one of the hidden spots in the brush. Having their own Halloween, a Halloween she knew she would one day have to graduate to, but that she didn't see the appeal of. Her Halloween was one of tradition, and of scary tales, and of a chance to look at the world as more magical than it is. The grown-up Halloween was just another night where a party happens, like any Friday or Saturday night. The thought depressed her.

"Looks like a real good time," he said. "I can't wait until we get invited to stuff like that."

"Really?"

"Yeah, don't you want to see what's next? I always want to see what's next."

"No," she said. "I never want to see what's next."

They tried a few more houses. Only one person answered.

"Sorry, kids, I'm on my way to bed," the woman who answered said, and shut the door before they could even finish their trick-or-treat.

"What is going on?" Esther said.

"Come on, Est. Can we go home now? Speaking of which, I should call my mom."

He pulled out his cell phone. Esther looked around. Between the streetlights and the big orange moon, the street was nearly as bright as day. So where were all the trick-or-treaters? Sure, the little kids would be done already, but where were the older kids? She wasn't the only one still going out. The streets should have had plenty of people. But they were alone, other than a few groups in the distance that all seemed to be hurrying, head down, rather than stopping at the houses.

"Gus, something isn't right."

"Est, I'm on the phone."

He waited with the phone to his ear for a bit and then shrugged, slipping it back into the belt of his costume.

"She's not picking up. Figures. She kind of loses track of the world when she works. Man, there were some movies I really wanted to see, and instead I'm out here not getting candy."

"Agustín, where are the other kids?"

He looked around.

"Ah, they're just . . . I don't know." He frowned. "That is weird. Where *are* the other kids? And why isn't anyone answering their door?" Esther could see the last twenty minutes finally sinking in with him. "This is definitely weird. Maybe I should try my mom again."

Down the street, she caught movement, a white flash. She squinted against the brightness of the streetlights and recognized the apple truck, slowly cruising toward them down the empty streets.

"Call her later," she said. "Let's head back this way." She took him by the hand, and they went back around the corner. They made it half a block before she realized she was still holding on to his hand.

16

THEY WERE MOST OF the way back down Meadow-lark, although Esther wasn't sure where they were going. Her house was out. If her parents caught her in costume like this, they would be furious. But she didn't feel safe out on the streets. She couldn't say what was wrong, but she felt a certainty that they needed to get back inside.

And then she knew where to go. The house on Spindrift with the haunted house in the backyard. The group of parents that threw a party and then took turns jumping out at the trick-or-treaters. They could go in there, be off the street for a bit, maybe have a chance to think through what to do next. It was only a couple blocks away.

She took those blocks at a jog, and Agustín followed her lead without question. He didn't want to be out here any more than she did. They jogged in silence, except for their huffing breaths. There were no costumed children walking up the garden paths, no friendly faces opening doors. The streets were empty.

No. Not quite empty. Somewhere behind them, though she never looked back, there was an ice cream truck full of apples, creeping slowly down the street. And if it caught them? She couldn't imagine. Or she could imagine many, many things, but she didn't want to. A whole variety of horrible fates, borrowed from every scary movie she had ever seen.

But never mind the truck. There was the house: 4391 Spindrift Court. The front windows were brightly lit, and she could hear music blaring inside. Beyond the garage, the side gate was open, with a sign saying: Haunted Maze. Free . . . If You Dare. They dared, gripping at the rotting wood of the garden gate as they passed through it. Black tarp led them into the maze.

Halloween sound effects played. Esther and Agustín jumped at the sound of a woman screaming from an old movie. (The actress screaming was named Maggie Rosenthal. She recorded that scream in 1967. Two years later, she retired from the movie business and moved back to Minnesota to become a geography teacher. She got married and had two children. After thirty years of teaching and fifteen years of retirement, Maggie passed away, surrounded by her loving family.)

But Esther and Agustín didn't know any of that, and the slow, inevitable passage of time wasn't what was scary about the sound effect. It was just a startling scream.

There were glow-in-the-dark skeletons in the haunted maze, and more fake cobwebs. But no one was jumping out at them. In fact, the haunted house seemed empty. Mr. Winchell was the neighborhood's true great artist of Halloween decorations. Esther only loved this house a little more because, well, free haunted house and people jumping out to scare you. Without the people, it was only a big tent, some tarps, and a few skeletons. And the sound effects CD, which had finished playing Maggie's screams and now was on to an electronic whirring sound that Esther thought might be intended to sound like a flying saucer.

They found themselves deposited back out on the other side of the yard without having seen a single other person at all.

"Okay, what the heck," said Agustín.

"I don't know what the heck," Esther said. "Let's go inside and find out."

Even with everything else that had happened, they felt as though they were doing something wrong when they walked through the front door into the adult side of the party. An upbeat rock song with a lot of bass shook the pictures on the walls. There were red plastic cups everywhere, and cupcakes shaped like jack-o'-lanterns. But mostly there were sleeping people.

An entire party of adults, sprawled asleep on the couch, on the floor, face-first into the snack table. Some of them had plates by their hands, or drinks spilled down their chests. Two of them had fallen asleep in a position that would have been horrifyingly embarrassing if they had been awake to know it was happening.

Esther and Agustín stepped over the man by the door, who had fallen asleep with the trick-or-treat bowl of candy in his hand, little foil-wrapped bars spilling onto his face.

"They're all breathing, right?" Esther said.

"Yeah, they're breathing fine," Agustín said. "They're just . . . they're asleep."

"Hey, wake up!" Esther shouted at the guy by the door, shaking his shoulder. Agustín did the same to a woman with a cupcake upside down on her lap, her hand still raised to her face where she had been about to put it. But neither of them moved at all.

"Oh man, are they all poisoned or something?" Agustín said.

Esther was already pulling out her cell phone, calling 9-1-1. Forget getting in trouble. This was an emergency. There was something very wrong, and she needed to get help for these people.

The line rang and rang. No one picked up. She tried it again. Nothing.

"9-1-1 isn't picking up," she said.

"What do you mean 9-1-1 isn't picking up? 9-1-1 picks up."

"I mean, 9-1-1 isn't picking up!"

Agustín swore and pulled out his cell phone, but he had the same result.

"9-1-1 always picks up," he shouted at his phone, but shouting didn't change the situation they were in.

And then that situation got worse. Artificial chimes playing a lurching waltz, with the notes just out of tune. They went to the doorway. The truck pulled up in front of the house. Queen of Halloween Apples. The horrible man she had met yesterday got out. His uniform and hair were as neat and spotless as before.

"Hey, kids," he called with a friendly wave. "I'm Dan. Dan Apel."

"I remember you," said Esther.

"Well, what seems to be the problem here?"

He strode up the walk, humming to himself, and poked his head inside. Esther and Agustín retreated farther into the house to keep away from him.

"Mmm," said Dan, with exaggerated concern. "Yeah, this seems like quite a bad situation you've gotten yourself into. It looks like all these folks are taking a nap, and you're in here bothering them. You shouldn't do that, you know. It's rude."

"Did you do this?" Esther said.

"Did I do this?" He laughed, actually slapping his knee. "Oh gosh, I'm not nearly powerful enough to do something like this. But I think I know who did. And I'll tell you what else, kids."

He cocked his head. His broad smile was exactly as perfect as it had been the day before, and exactly as false.

"I think whoever did this is only getting started. You

should run on home to your parents now." His voice became cold even as his toothy smile held. "It's going to be a long night. A very, very long night."

He chuckled and muttered to himself, "Did I do this? Imagine that," then walked, whistling, back to his truck, leaving Esther and Agustín alone with the unconscious adults.

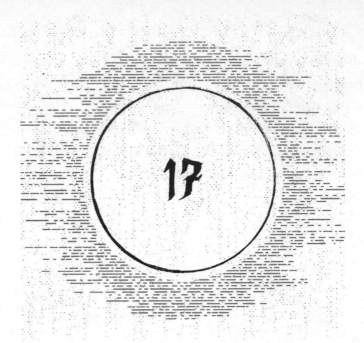

"MOM! DAD!"

As soon as the truck had turned the corner Esther started sprinting for home. Whatever was happening was serious and it was bad and she needed her parents.

Her house was silent. There was no sign of her parents in the living room or the kitchen. She ran into the back hall, still shouting for them. The door to their bedroom was open, the lights were on. She could see her dad's feet in socks and the toes of her mom's shoes through the doorway.

"Mom? Dad?" Quieter. A question, not a call. She stepped into the room, afraid of what she might find. Her parents were lying on the bed, fully clothed. They were breathing gently, her dad making a soft wheeze with each exhale. They were fast asleep.

She grabbed her dad's foot. Shook her mom hard by the

shoulders. Clapped right between their heads. Neither of them even mumbled or turned over.

"They're not waking up. Why aren't they waking up?" she said.

"It's like the people at the party," Agustín said. "That weirdo did something to them."

"What could do this? What could do this?" she asked over and over, as though there were someone who might be able to tell her.

Without a great deal of hope, she tried 9-1-1 again on her phone. Ringing and ringing and nothing at all. Agustín, meanwhile, dialed his house again, then his mother's cell phone.

"She's still not answering," he said. "She might be at the workshop, but . . ."

"I'm sure she's fine," said Esther, although she was not sure of that, and Agustín knew she wasn't sure.

If her parents couldn't help her, then the next rung down the ladder was her brother, Ben. Not the most responsible teenager, but older than her by four years, a senior in high school. She checked his room. There was no sign of him. He had been meeting up with his friends. She tried texting him, but he didn't reply. Ben was never not looking at his phone, so he must be really distracted to not see her texts.

With no one left who could take care of her, it occurred to her finally that there was someone else more helpless than her.

"Sharon," she said, and ran to Sharon's room. It would

be fine. Sharon would be in her bed (having recently graduated from her crib), tucked in, sleeping. But what if she couldn't be woken up?

It was worse than that. "Oh my god," Esther said.

Sharon was gone.

"Let's search around the house," Agustín said. "She probably just got freaked out and went looking for help."

They went through the entire house, plus the backyard and the garage, shouting Sharon's name.

"Nowhere," Esther said. "She's nowhere. My parents are asleep and can't wake up. My brother is out who knows where, and my baby sister is gone."

She felt blank. Not afraid, just nothing at all. She would have to give up. Sit here and wait until everything got better.

There was a knock at the door. A soft, sharp tapping. They turned to the windows but couldn't see anything through them.

Slowly, Esther approached the door, with Agustín immediately behind. She cracked open the door.

There was a child in a dinosaur costume. The costume had stains all over it, and one of the big dinosaur eyes was missing. She couldn't see the child's face in the shadow of the dinosaur mask.

"Are you lost?" she said.

The child made a buzzing, clicking sound, like an insect.

"There's something wrong with that kid," Agustín said.

The buzzing from the trick-or-treater got louder.

She was about to shut the door when she heard a different sound.

"Mom? Mom? Please, Mom, wake up. Mom!"

A girl's voice from down the street. Esther hesitated a moment, eyeing the buzzing creature in her doorway. But there was another person out there, awake and going through the same horrible experience that she was. She threw open the door and sprinted past the dinosaur costume and down the walk. The trick-or-treater didn't move, although it made a series of loud clicks as Agustín followed Esther past it.

They made it to the sidewalk, and Esther paused, unsure of which direction to go.

"Help!" the voice shouted, and Esther ran toward it.

There was a minivan parked on the street, and a girl bent over the driver's seat.

"Hey!" Esther said as she ran up.

The girl turned. She was holding the hand of Mrs. Min, who was slumped in the driver's seat, asleep.

"Oh god, not you," Sasha Min said.

18

"WHAT ARE YOU DOING HERE?" Sasha said. She was wearing a baseball uniform and had black stripes painted under her eyes.

"I live right there," Esther said.

"Oh," Sasha said. "Oh. Well. Okay." Her desire to ignore Esther was overwhelmed by her panic. "My mom won't wake up. Can you help me?"

Esther and Agustín went to take a look. Mrs. Min was exactly like the Golds had been. Peacefully sleeping, breathing normally, but completely unable to be shaken out of sleep. Not reacting to even shouts or hard pokes.

"She was supposed to pick me up after trick-or-treating," Sasha said. "But when I got here, she was asleep, and I couldn't wake her up."

"You go trick-or-treating?" Esther said.

"Well yeah," Sasha said. "Whatever. That's not the point. My mom's in trouble. Help me."

"I'm trying, Sasha, but I'm not a doctor, and since I'm betting you tried calling 9-1-1 first, you know there's not a doctor coming anytime soon."

Sasha looked like she wanted to cry, but she managed to force it into a glare at Esther instead.

"You're a jerk. Go away, I need to help my mom."

Esther felt bad about how she had handled this. "Sasha," she said, trying to keep her voice quiet and gentle, "I know this is scary."

"You don't know anything. Go away."

"I'm scared too. My parents won't wake up. And my baby sister is missing. And no one is picking up the phone, and we seem to be alone here. Let's be honest. I don't like you. You don't like me. I don't even know why. We just don't. But we need to find help. And it'll be easier to do that together."

Sasha bit her lip, looked down at the street.

"Whatever, sure," she said. "Let's find help."

"Great, if you two are done arguing about whether you want to argue, I think we should start moving," Agustín said. "Or maybe you forgot buzzy kid back there."

"Buzzy kid?" Sasha said.

"Doesn't matter," Esther quickly interjected. Sasha was panicked enough. "If no one's outside, let's start knocking on doors again. Even houses with the lights off. Someone has to be up still." She paused, reconsidering. "At least I really hope so."

They moved systematically down the block, knocking on every door. No answers at any of them. Right when Esther was starting to think there wasn't another person left awake in the town, a woman swung open her door after three knocks. It was one of the houses with all of its front lights off, and no decorations.

"Do I look like I'm open for trick-or-treating?" the woman said. "And what time is it? You should be ashamed for bothering good people at this hour."

"I'm sorry, ma'am," Sasha said, in a different voice than Esther had ever heard. It was a "talking to grown-ups" voice; deferential, polite, but also deeper and less kid-like. "We're having an emergency, and we need help."

"It's late," the woman said. "And I'm tired. I've been yawning for hours. How late is it?" She lifted her arm as though to check her watch, but seemed to run out of energy halfway up and dropped it again without looking. "You kids go to bed. Stop bothering your neighbors."

"You're not listening," Esther said. "Our parents are in trouble. There are lots of people in trouble. Help us, please."

"Kids think they know everything," the woman said, swinging the door shut, then shouting through the closed door, "Go to bed! And don't knock again, because I'm going to bed too."

Esther met Agustín's eyes, sharing a moment of despair, and then looked over at Sasha, who was struggling to keep it together. Seeing Sasha like that made Esther want to be strong.

"Okay, not a problem," she said. "Or, yes, a problem, but we need to keep moving."

"There's something horribly wrong going on here," Sasha said. "That woman wasn't acting normal. None of this is normal."

"Hate to side against you, Est," Agustín said. "But Sasha's right. This isn't normal. I don't think knocking on doors will work."

Even though she didn't disagree with anything that either of them were saying, she was furious at Agustín for taking Sasha's side.

"Okay, fine," she said. "Then what do you think we should do? Just go back to Sasha's original idea? Running around screaming help until our throats give out?"

"Are you making fun of me for trying to help my mother?" Sasha said, her fury shaking her out of her panic.

"Est," Agustín said.

"No, no," said Esther. "I think it was a great idea. Let's do it more. Here I go." She went to the middle of the street and screamed at the top of her lungs: "Help! Help us, someone! If I keep screaming, will you come help us?"

"I'm leaving," Sasha said. "You're both jerks."

"Don't go," Agustín said. "We have to stick together."

"Oh help me!" Esther continued to shout. "I'm a helpless child. Won't somebody assist little me?"

Sasha rolled her eyes and started to walk away.

"Hey!" a new voice said. "What are you kids screaming about? Are you in trouble?"

They all turned. Mr. Gabler was standing on his front lawn, holding his basket of toothbrushes and mini-toothpaste tubes.

"Esther," he said, his brow furrowed. "You sounded terrified. What's the emergency?"

Esther couldn't believe it. An adult, awake and offering to help her. She wanted to cry, right there in the middle of the street.

Instead, she steadied her voice and forced herself to say, "Oh, Mr. Gabler! I am so glad to see you. May we come in?"

MR. GABLER LED THEM into the kitchen. On the counter was a pile of that week's newspapers. He frowned and pushed them aside. Esther saw a headline about the robbery of the collector in the hills and thought of her conversation with Agustín in his front yard. Had that only been a day ago? It already felt like it existed on the other side of some impossible divide in her life.

"Now tell me what is going on," Mr. Gabler said. "And please be quiet. Mrs. Gabler has already gone to bed, and I don't want any of you waking her up."

"Have you tried to wake her up?" Sasha asked.

"Why would I try to wake her up once she's gone to bed? I should be in bed too, I felt very sleepy, but when I lay down, I got poked by this in my pocket." He held up a small, sharp stone. "Not sure how it got there. The surprise woke me right up, I guess. Now what are you doing here?"

Esther told him about her sleeping parents and Mrs. Min sleeping in the car, about Sharon going missing, the party full of sleeping people who could not be woken up, the doors that no one was answering, the white trucks with men inside that seemed to want to do them harm, her brother being out at a party, and finally remembering to include that 9-1-1 wasn't picking up, that no one was picking up, that phones seemed to be useless. She only left out the buzzing trick-or-treaters in their ragged and dirty costumes. She didn't know what words to use to describe them, how she would get anyone to believe her.

Mr. Gabler listened to all of this with remarkable patience, his arms crossed, only raising his eyebrows at her missing sister and at 9-1-1 not working. When she had finished, he stood there processing it for a second in silence. Then he uncrossed his arms and put his hands on the counter.

"Well," he said. "I don't know what's going on that would make you think you could make up stuff like that to anyone, let alone a busy adult who you barely know."

"I'm not making any of it up," she started to protest, but he waved her to silence.

"But if any part of what you're saying is true, if your sister is really missing, then we need to get the police involved. And if you turn out to be making it up, that will be a bad mess for you. Not my problem, though."

"Did you listen to what she was saying?" Sasha said. "No one is picking up at 9-1-1."

"I heard," he said. "But maybe their number just went down for a couple minutes, or they were experiencing heavy call volume. Or maybe you made that up too. For your sake, I hope it wasn't that last one."

He pulled out his cell phone, held down the 9, and waited for the beep. Even though Esther knew it wouldn't work, she felt some comfort being around Mr. Gabler. He was so utterly boring, so completely without adventure, that he seemed the antidote to all the strangeness of the night so far.

"I'm looking forward to having you out of my home. Come to me at this time of night telling me a story like that." He shook his head. "I always liked you, Esther. You seemed like a good kid."

He stood with his phone to his ear for a full minute.

"Huh," he said. "It's just ringing."

"That's what we told you!" Esther said.

"It's the truth, Mr. Gabler," Agustín said.

Mr. Gabler tried again, and there was still no answer.

"Okay," he said, sounding less angry and more concerned. "Here's what we'll do. Come on."

He led them back out of the kitchen to the front door.

"Let me have a talk with your parents. I'm sure everything's fine. I'll walk you back to your house and then we'll get this settled."

Esther realized that the only thing that would make someone as boring as Mr. Gabler believe was seeing for himself, so she nodded politely and said, "Sure, Mr. Gabler."

Outside, the moon was huge and orange on the horizon. The stars twinkled. A cool wind blew, autumn flexing its muscles slightly even in warm California.

"I think we can get this straightened out with a quick word with your parents," Mr. Gabler said as they walked, to no one in particular. There were no cars on the street. No people. Esther wondered if Mr. Gabler noticed how desolate the entire neighborhood had become. How quiet. Not even the blue light of television flickering in front windows or from second-floor bedrooms.

And maybe they would get back to her house, and her parents would be waiting at the door, worried. They would yell at her, probably ground her, and she would love that. She wanted nothing more in this moment than her dad to say, "What in the world were you thinking?", for her mom to say, "Are you trying to punish us? Is that it?" with pained disappointment in her voice.

Instead she heard engines. In perfect synchronization, the two white ice cream trucks turned onto the street and approached, side by side. They drove at exactly the same speed, an oncoming wall of headlights and metal.

"Uh, Mr. Gabler," Esther said.

"Oh look," he said. "Here's some other people now. Maybe they've seen something."

"Mr. Gabler, no," Agustín said.

But Mr. Gabler was already waving at the trucks. The two trucks turned toward each other, barely missing a collision and skidding to a halt in a V-shape blocking the street.

Dan hopped out of his truck, and Ed Pumken slumped out of the other. Ed held his hat crumpled in his hand. Dan, as though to show him up, took off his hat, carefully brushed it and fixed any indentations, then put it neatly back on his head.

"Hi, is there a problem, sir?" Dan said to Mr. Gabler.

"Seems these kids are having some kind of emergency. Do you have a cell phone? Mine isn't getting through to the police."

Dan made an exaggerated frown, a parody of a concerned citizen.

"Oh no, I'm afraid I don't have a phone on me. Ed, do you have a phone?"

Ed laughed, an ugly bark.

"No phone either, I guess," Dan said. "I apologize for that. But I believe I might be able to help you with the children."

"Yeah?" Mr. Gabler said. The vibe these two were putting out was starting to make him suspicious. He backed up protectively in front of Esther and the others.

"Oh yes," Dan said. "You see, I told them to go home already. It seems they did not. Always a pity when children are so disobedient, you know?"

"Rotten kids," Ed said.

"Crude, but not unfair," Dan said, nodding at his brother. "You see, it is getting late. It will continue to be late. It will stay late for a long, long time. And Mr. Gabler, if I can be honest with you . . ."

"How do you know my name?" Mr. Gabler took a step back, unconsciously spreading his arms a little to cover the kids behind him.

"Mr. Gabler, it would have been better if you had remained in your home, yawned a bit, and then gone to bed. It would have been so much simpler for you to have dreamed through it like all the rest."

Dan opened up the side of his truck. There was a pile of gleaming, perfect apples, red as the inside of an eyelid, red as the tip of a tongue, red as a fresh paper cut. He grabbed one off the top. Ed smirked in anticipation.

"But it's okay!" Dan said, in his friendly salesman voice. "We always keep our options open. Just for folks like you. In fact, I've prepared quite a special surprise."

He held up the apple. "Healthiest fruit in the world," he said. "They've done studies, you know. No substitute for an apple." There was something terribly wrong with the apple. Its skin rippled and bulged, like there were worms writhing inside. Narrow slits broke open in the skin, and viciously sharp razor blades blossomed out of the apple, like terrible flowers, until the entire apple was bristling with deadly edges.

"I've prepared quite a surprise indeed," Dan said. He tossed the razor-blade apple from hand to hand. The razors sank into his skin, and his hands went wet. His smile did not waver once.

20

ESTHER DIDN'T KNOW what to do in this situation. Nothing in her life's experience had told her what to do when a man started tossing around an apple studded with razor blades.

Ed laughed at the group's panic, as they backed up to the side fence of the house along the street. He waved his arms at them, revealing yellow pit stains.

"Boogey, boogey, boogey," he shouted, and laughed again.

Dan, his fingers red and wet, wound up and threw. The apple shot like a bullet, no arc, pure speed, and—*thwick*—embedded in the wooden fence behind them. Already he had grabbed another apple from his pile, and it was sprouting razor blades from beneath its skin, making a soft, squishy sound as it transformed.

"Back to my house," Mr. Gabler said, and they started

to run in that direction, but two more apples cut them off, popping into the fence right in front of a startled Agustín, who stopped so abruptly he fell backward into Esther. She caught him and pushed him back upright. Without talking about it, they turned and ran the other way, trying to rush past the trucks, but an apple swished right above Esther's head, and they had to stop again.

"You had a chance to leave," Dan said. "I'm afraid you chose not to. We all have decisions in life, and we have to live with the choices we made. Or no longer live with those choices, as the case may be." He clutched razor apples in both hands. His smile was no longer cool and professional, but had lolled open into a toothy sneer.

"What do you want?" Mr. Gabler shouted.

In answer, Dan set off a flurry of razor apples, landing everywhere on the fence behind them except where they stood. Despite all of the apples he had thrown, the pile in his truck seemed no smaller than before.

"Alright," Mr. Gabler said. "Okay. Alright. Here's what we'll do." He turned and, in a single fluid movement, kicked the fence with a startling amount of power. Weighed down by all of the apples, the fence tumbled flat. "Run!"

Esther didn't let herself think about what they were doing, because she knew that their chances were slim, and doubt could easily overtake her, leaving her frozen and in easy reach of Dan Apel's nightmarish stock of weapons. Instead she leapt over the razor-studded fence and ran into the neighbor's backyard.

The house was the one across the street from her own. It wasn't until she was fleeing through the woman's yard that Esther realized how little she knew of this neighbor, or any of her neighbors. Outside of a couple houses right next to her own, she didn't even know what her neighbors looked like, let alone their names. The old woman whose backyard she was currently sprinting through had only ever been an object of derision in the Gold family, because of the lady's tendency to call the city about any tiny perceived violation of code.

For instance, her father had once gone outside to find a police officer writing a ticket to one of the Gold family's own cars, parked in their own driveway.

"Got a call from a neighbor, complaining," the police officer had said. "This car is blocking a driveway."

"It's our car," her dad said. "In our driveway."

Even the police officer could see that this was going to be a tricky one to explain to a court, and so he retreated into a look of blank authority.

"It's blocking the driveway. We got a call from a neighbor."

This interaction repeated a few times before the cop couldn't deliver his own argument with conviction and left. The old woman across the street had watched all this from her window, and thrust the curtains shut in frustration when no ticket was issued.

Now Esther was running for her life through the old woman's backyard. Apples studded with blades whizzed over their heads. As the fruit struck, they spat up dirt clods from the lawn and sprays of pebbles from the path, embedded into the back deck, shattered the stucco on the side of the house. The apples came impossibly fast, no pause between volleys. One deadly missile after another.

"Can you all hop a fence?" Mr. Gabler yelled as they approached the wooden barrier between them and the next neighbor's yard.

"Yeah," Agustín said.

"Yes," Sasha shouted.

Esther had never hopped a fence before and was clumsy under the best of circumstances. She couldn't believe that apparently Mr. Gabler and even Sasha could hop a fence and she couldn't. But she could see that this fence was firmly embedded into cinder blocks. It would be difficult to knock down, would slow them at a time when any slowness was fatal. She would have to get over the top somehow.

"Definitely," she lied.

She hit the fence at a run. She knew that if she swung a leg over, she would get stuck in an awkward straddle, and she didn't have the upper-body strength to push herself fully over. So in a move that she would never have tried in any situation where she was not fleeing for her life, she flopped herself over in a flailing somersault, landing hard on her back on the other side. Her head just missed the cinder blocks holding the fence up.

"You said you could climb it," Mr. Gabler said, vaulting the fence with a surprising, well-practiced grace.

She scrambled up. Her neck was sore, but everything else seemed to be working okay.

"Well I made it over, didn't I?" she groaned.

A truck revved to life behind them, then another.

No time for discussion. Again they ran. She vaguely knew the yard they were fleeing through, having been friends for a brief time with the girl who lived here, Susan Watkins. But Susan's family had moved out after only a couple years, and the house had been occupied since by a series of increasingly careless renters. This yard was nothing like the paragon of tidiness they had just passed through. The grass of this yard stretched yellow and dry up to their knees. There were hidden dangers within the brittle lawn, bricks and bottles invisible until a toe smacked painfully against them. The back deck consisted of only a fire pit that had not been cleaned in years and two lawn chairs made of ancient plastic strips manufactured in a defiantly ugly yellow.

The apple truck burst through the fence behind them, tires bouncing over the cinder block base like it was nothing. It looked like a simple ice cream truck, but physics appeared meaningless to it. Dan hung out the window. He zipped two apples at them and laughed. One sliced through a lawn chair, and the ugly yellow plastic twanged into two.

The barrier to the next yard was not a fence, but a wall. Concrete blocks. Having gained some confidence from making it over the last fence, Esther let the momentum of her run carry her up the side and off the top. Her landing was complicated by a row of rose bushes planted under the wall, which caught her body about as well as rose bushes could. The pain was immediate and overwhelming, but she didn't have time to let it slow her down. She pulled herself off the bush and ran again, covered in little red spots where the thorns had gotten her.

"Let me help you next time," Agustín called.

"I'm doing it. I'm fine," she said. No one else could make her graceful or give her experience hopping fences that everyone else in the world seemed to mysteriously just have, so she would have to keep using sheer adrenaline to get her over. She started to sprint again, and then came to a skidding halt to keep from falling into the water.

A swimming pool took up most of the yard. Esther's left foot half hung over the side, and she teetered. There was a blue-gray diving board, hanging at an unsafe angle off its rusted base. An overgrown orange tree leaned over the pool, bursting with fruit, much of which had fallen into the water. The deep end was a bobbing carpet of leaves and oranges. She managed to pull herself back and cut to the right. The rest of the group had cut left, so they ran on either side of the pool toward the next yard. The reflected light from the pool's surface made ripples over their running bodies.

Bam. The truck blew through the concrete wall as if it were papier-mâché. Not a dent or a scratch. Dan flicked three more apples out of the driver's-side window, which buzzed past the runners, whipping into the orange tree. A thick branch was neatly severed from the trunk and fell, laden with ripe fruit, into the water.

Esther was at the next wall. This one was taller. She went for it. Everything around her turned white. She had popped

114

her jaw on the top. Her vision came back to her. She fell over the other side. Her face ached. Fortunately, she did not land in any thorns. But the yard held something even more unwelcome.

Ed's truck had torn through the side gate, and he was parked in the middle of the yard, cutting off their path forward. They came panting to a stop and looked around for an escape route. The wall exploded behind them, and the other truck was in the yard too. Surrounded once again. Esther closed her eyes, waiting for that buzzing sound and the pain that would come after. But Dan didn't throw another apple. He merely watched with that awful smile, his legs up on the dashboard and his neatly manicured hands behind his head.

Ed got out of his truck with an exasperated huff, rattling up the side panel to reveal a huge pile of orange pumpkins, orange as infection, orange as guts, orange as week-old roadkill. He clamped his grubby hand around a pumpkin's cartoonishly green and twisted stem.

"Those have knives in them too?" Esther asked.

"My apples have razor blades," Dan corrected, looking furious again. "Not knives. Come on, they tell stories about me. Get the details right."

"Sorry. Those pumpkins full of knives like your knife boy over there?" Esther corrected herself.

Dan turned red, but Ed smiled in appreciation for the joke at his brother's expense.

"Nah," he said. "Ain't you ever seen a jack-o'-lantern?"

The pumpkin Ed was holding heaved and morphed, and then the front of it split. Two triangle eyes, a triangle nose, and a wide wicked grin. Before they could react to that, the inside of the jack-o'-lantern sparked alight, a fire so hot it was nearly clear, then the entire pumpkin burst into violent flame. Ed made a quick twist of the wrist and flung it at their feet. The pumpkin exploded into a pool of raging fire, the heat distorting the air around them.

"Through the house," Esther said, already running. If they stayed where they were, they'd be fried. The others followed her through the back door. In the living room, two men she did not recognize but who had been her neighbors for much of her life were sitting in front of the TV. Both of them were fast asleep, one's head on the other's shoulder. The TV showed flickering blue lines, the only light in the house. The walls seemed alive in the wavering blue light. Esther and the others ran past the television and through to the front door, across the street, on to the house on the other side of the cul-de-sac. Esther desperately turned the knob of the front door. It was locked. Only Take One! Don't Be Naughty! said a sign on the door, with an arrow pointing to a bowl. The bowl was still heaped high with candy. Not a trick-or-treater in sight.

The pair of trucks came roaring out from either side of the house they had just fled and turned to pincer in on the group at the door. Dan held a razor apple. Ed held a jack-o'-lantern already engulfed in flames.

"Let me," Mr. Gabler said.

He grabbed the door handle, pulled up on it, and slammed his shoulder into the edge of the door farthest from the hinges. It popped open.

"How did you learn to do that?" Sasha said as they ran into the entryway. The house was full of knickknacks, old-fashioned rotary phones, glass bells printed with names of foreign countries, ceramic figurines of children doing old-timey activities.

"I wasn't always a dentist, you know," Mr. Gabler replied. He looked like he wasn't interested in elaborating on that. They hustled through the kitchen, past a woman snoring at the counter, and into the backyard, where the sound of the truck engines was getting louder by the second. They only had moments before they would be once again surrounded.

"Okay, to the right. Let's get back to Mr. Gabler's house," Esther said.

They went right. Over the fence. This one Esther took with something close to ease, only banging her ankle on the top of it as she swung over. She was getting okay at this.

Another swimming pool, this one covered for the coming winter. Then a yard that was landscaped in a clever way that separated the small yard into sections of garden connected by a meandering path, having the effect of making the yard seem much larger than it was and also making fleeing through it a nightmare of dead ends and obstacles. Then her next-door neighbor's yard. She didn't know anything about her neighbors other than their names and faces, and their adorable beagle named Romeo who lived in the front yard. Almost certainly this backyard was full of stray balls and frisbees her family had lost over the fence into the overgrown bushes, never retrieved for fear of having to bother the neighbors.

She led them over the fence, darting across the street before the trucks could turn the corner, and over the fence again into Mr. Gabler's yard.

"Alright, inside," she said.

They ran through the sliding back door of the Gabler house, and shut it. Then, working together, they did their best to push furniture against doors and windows, leaning the couch up against the front window, until they created as much of a barricade as they could. Of course, the trucks could just smash through those walls like they were nothing, but that hadn't happened yet. They could hear the engines idling outside, seemingly happy to let their prey stay holed up.

After this flurry of activity, they stood in the Gabler family dining room, the furniture all rearranged, the table wedged under the front door.

"Okay," said Agustín. "What now?"

"I guess we wait to see what they do next," Esther said. She looked at Mr. Gabler, the adult, to see if he approved or disapproved of this plan, but he just shrugged.

"I guess we do," he said.

AT FIRST THEY STOOD ALERT by the doors and windows, waiting for the attack. But nothing happened. The trucks idled threateningly outside, but neither of the men seemed interested in getting in, merely in preventing them from getting out. So eventually they left Mr. Gabler to keep an eye on the door, and the three of them went into the kitchen for a late-night snack. Fleeing for their lives had worked up their appetite.

"Turkey in the fridge, bread on the counter. If you make a mess, you clean it up," Mr. Gabler said. He sat in the one chair in the living room that hadn't been conscripted into the barricade.

They wolfed down their sandwiches, not noticing until then how hungry they had been. Esther was unsure how much time had passed since her last meal. The measurement of time had become difficult, and she wasn't sure she trusted the red digits of the clock on the stove. Sasha tried turning on the TV, but there wasn't any signal coming through.

A few hours passed, with no change and no movement from outside. The tension within them unwound a bit. Still present and accounted for, but not so intense as to make other thought impossible. Esther even found herself getting bored. She went into the upstairs bathroom and looked in the mirror. The gory face of a killer looked back at her.

She peeled off the wounds, leaving them in a stack by the sink, and wiped off the makeup using remover that presumably belonged to Mrs. Gabler, until it was only her face, the face of a thirteen-year-old girl, looking back. She thought about what that face would look like when she was twenty, or thirty, or even as impossibly old as forty. Where would the wrinkles go? Here at the corners of her eyes? Here on her cheeks?

The distance between her face and any face she might have in the future seemed an astonishing and impossible gap, and she wondered how it ever happened to anyone.

She came back out of the bathroom and leaned over the landing. Sasha was in the living room downstairs, flicking idly through a dental trade journal.

"Where's Agustín?" Esther said.

Sasha rolled her eyes. "I don't know. Up there, I think?"

Esther looked around. One bedroom door was closed. She assumed that Mrs. Gabler was sleeping an unwakeable sleep in there. The other bedroom's door was open.

"Agustín?" Esther said into the dark doorway.

"Yeah. I'm in here."

He was sitting on the bed, looking out the window. Esther supposed he was looking at the moon. Orange and huge and low to the horizon, it cast everything in the dark room in the faint hue of a pumpkin. She sat down next to him.

"How are you doing?" she said. She didn't know how else to talk about everything they had just gone through.

"It's not moving," he said.

"What?"

"The moon. Hasn't moved. It's been hours."

She looked again. He was right. The moon was exactly where it had been when they started trick-or-treating.

"That can't be good," she said.

"I told you Halloween sucked."

"Shut up, it's not Halloween's fault."

"None of this is real, right?" he said. "This is just a dream we're having?"

She pinched his arm.

"Ow!"

"I think if we were talking in a dream we'd know. It wouldn't feel like this. It would feel different."

"Maybe," he said.

They sat in silence for a while. The silence was comfortable. It was almost welcome after all the noise and panic of the chase.

In that silence, she found herself thinking about something she had been turning over in her mind for the last few weeks.

"Gus, do you think we'll still be friends like this in high school?"

He looked at her. Their eyes had adjusted enough to the darkness that they both were visible, but in soft focus. Fainter, less flawed versions of what they really looked like.

"Yeah. I mean, sure. Why wouldn't we be? We're still friends in junior high."

"I feel like high school might be different. Or . . ." She put her face in her hands. "I'm not making sense. I just don't know what high school is going to be like. It's a blank for me."

"I think it'll be what we decide to make it. That's what my mom always says. She says fate isn't real, that we decide what happens in our own lives. Like we'll stay friends if we want to stay friends. And we want to stay friends, right?"

She frowned. "People say that the future is what you make of it. But I don't think that's true. I think it just comes, and maybe you get some choices, but above all the future is change. You can't control change."

"Man." He turned to face her. "You're really freaked out about getting older, huh?"

She turned to face him too. "I guess I just see how getting older works with my brother, and my parents, and my grandma Debbie. Each year everything becomes more complicated and less easy."

Then they were facing each other, and silent again, and now the silence wasn't comfortable. In the unnatural orange light, he had never looked less like himself, but still she recognized the person she had spent the most time with in the last few years. This wasn't a dream. If this were a dream, she might be able to say the things that she was realizing she wanted to say. But she couldn't say that stuff here, in the real world, where it was the two of them in their three-dimensional, oxygen-needing bodies, waiting awkwardly through the silence.

He smiled and indicated the trucks lurking outside. "You really think we're gonna make it to high school, anyway?"

And in that moment, she knew she was going to say it after all. Here in this real world, right in this real moment, she was going to start talking to him about it.

But when she opened her mouth, the window in the room collapsed inward in a violent explosion of glass, and instead of words she only screamed.

They jumped up off the bed, backing away from the broken window.

Click. Click. Click. Insect legs. A whirring.

A shadow in the window, against the orange bright of the moon. The shadow was a trick-or-treater in the white sheet of an old-fashioned ghost costume. The sheet was torn and stained with red-brown splotches. The trick-or-treater tilted its head and buzzed at them.

"Run," said Agustín, but Esther was already running.

22

ESTHER SPRINTED DOWN the dark and unfamiliar hallway with the buzzing of the ghost trick-or-treater in the room behind them, like a chorus of every angry wasp that ever chased a well-meaning child.

"Sasha! Mr. Gabler," she shouted as she made it to the stairs and saw dust plume out from the fireplace in the living room below. Scuffed tennis shoes emerged from the chimney, attached to the trick-or-treater in a ragged dinosaur costume.

"We're here," said Mr. Gabler from the kitchen. "Can you make it to us safely?"

"Yes," said Esther, not at all sure they could. She looked at Agustín and opened her mouth, but before she could say anything, there was a blur from behind her. She turned to see the trick-or-treater in the ghost costume scrambling at them on all fours down the hallway, a sickening whirring sound coming from its throat.

Without thinking, she took Agustín's hand and hurried them both down the stairs. The dinosaur, still with one arm in the chimney, lunged at her, clicking wildly. She dodged away from it and into the kitchen. Mr. Gabler and Sasha were sitting on the floor. Sasha was absolutely determined not to cry, a determination so absolute she was in tears from the effort. Mr. Gabler looked confused and angry. He held a kitchen knife in front of him.

"Okay," he said. "This is enough." He stood up and faced the living room. The dinosaur was lurching toward them, leaving ash footprints on the carpet. The ghost ran directly into the railing at the top of the stairs, hitting it hard and flopping over, landing in a pile in the middle of the living room. Then it rose, a little bent from the impact, and continued coming for them.

"I don't know who . . . what you are," said Mr. Gabler. "But I bet a knife works on you just the same." He put one arm out to shield the children. "So come on, give it your best shot."

Which was when two dirty, costumed arms smashed through the kitchen window behind him and pulled him outside. With a single shout of surprise, he was gone.

"Mr. Gabler!" called Esther, but there was no answer. A trick-or-treater looked in from outside the broken window, wearing a cheap rubber mask of a pirate captain with an eye patch and a big grin. The pirate buzzed, and the dinosaur and ghost buzzed back at it. The two intruders were at the kitchen door now.

"What do we do?" said Agustín.

Esther didn't know. So she moved without knowing what she would do next. She put down her head and charged the two trick-or-treaters at the kitchen door and barreled through them. Unprepared for the velocity of a thirteen-year-old full of adrenaline, the two trick-or-treaters were shoved aside. Agustín and Sasha sprinted after her.

Esther made for the front door. As she turned toward it, the front door opened. For a moment it felt like her sheer desire to escape had cleared a path, but then she saw what had actually opened the door. A trick-or-treater dressed as a clown. This one didn't buzz. This one laughed, a sickly, wheezing giggle.

She screamed, pivoted, and went upstairs with Agustín and Sasha scrambling behind her. This, Esther knew as a longtime viewer of horror movies, was the wrong move. There was no escape upstairs. But there did not seem to be escape anywhere, and at least upstairs didn't have a scary clown. Yet.

Unwilling to go back into the bedroom where they had first been attacked, she instead opened the door of the master bedroom. There was Mrs. Gabler, sprawled on her back with her mouth wide open, snoring.

"Mrs. Gabler, wake up!" Esther tried.

"But they can't—" said Agustín as he and Sasha caught up.

"It seemed worth trying." Esther slammed the door shut and started to look for something to barricade it with. There wasn't much furniture. The Gablers were minimalist in their decorating style. The only possible choice for a barricade was a dresser.

"Help me," she said, pulling at it, and Sasha and Agustín went around to push. But earthquakes are common in California, so the Gablers had wisely anchored the dresser to the wall.

"Oh no," said Sasha.

"Oh no," said Agustín.

"Aaaah," screamed Esther again. This last time because the door had slammed open. There was the ghost, and there was the pirate, and there was the dinosaur, and behind them the wheezing clown. "Ahhhh!" she added for good measure.

She tried to think about what a person in a horror movie would do in this situation. But what a person in a horror movie would do in this situation was die, and she didn't want to do that. So instead she kept screaming. A person in a horror movie would do that too.

There was a click behind her. She whirled to see what new terror had arrived. Instead she saw the familiar face of Mr. Gabler. His face was freshy bruised, and he clenched the kitchen knife between his teeth. For a moment, it seemed to Esther that he was flying, but she realized that he had climbed the stucco wall of his house and was now deftly jimmying open the locked window. Once the window was open, he smoothly popped the screen out and was inside.

He twisted his ankle as he landed and winced, but he took the knife from his mouth and waved it at the monsters at the door.

"Back off!" he said, emphasizing the words with stabs at

the air. The trick-or-treaters buzzed louder than ever, but they didn't come any closer. For the first time, they seemed unsure. Mr. Gabler roared and threw himself forward. All four trick-or-treaters melted away into the air. Esther assumed they must have scurried off, but she couldn't be sure. They were there, solid and threatening, and then they were completely gone.

Esther and the other three stood in silence, letting their breath settle back into their bodies. After a minute, the three of them turned to look at Mr. Gabler, still standing at the bedroom door with the knife, rubbing his ankle.

"How did you climb the wall like that?" said Agustín.

"Yeah, and how did you know how to open a locked window like that?" said Esther.

"And where did you learn to use a knife like that?" said Sasha.

Mr. Gabler adjusted his glasses and sighed. "I wasn't always a dentist, you know."

23

"HELLO IN THERE," called a familiar voice from outside. They gathered around the window, which Mr. Gabler quickly shut again and relocked. Esther thought again of how easily he had unlocked it from the outside. Where in the world did someone as boring as Mr. Gabler learn how to do that? It was starting to seem that the adult world was full of more secrets and surprises than even her most favorite horror movies.

"Yes, you dummies in the house. I'm talking to you," called the same voice again. It was Dan, a bullhorn up to his mouth. He spotted them in the window and gave them his biggest customer-service smile and a friendly wave. "There you are. Thought maybe you had met a truly unfortunate end at the hands of our friends." He frowned thoughtfully. "Although technically they don't have hands, exactly." Back to the same perfect smile. "But close enough."

"You don't scare us," Esther lied loudly through the window.

"Yes we do," answered Dan truthfully. "But we don't have to anymore. You could surrender. Then this would all be over. It doesn't have to be unpleasant. You could just go to sleep. Like your wife, Mr. Gabler. Doesn't she look peaceful?"

Mrs. Gabler snorted and rolled over, pulling all of the covers off one side of the bed.

"She always did burrito herself in the sheets," muttered Mr. Gabler.

"No deal," shouted Agustín. "Go away."

"Ah well. Her Majesty won't be happy about all this fuss. But we'll have it cleaned up before she arrives. See you soon." Dan shut off the megaphone and disappeared into the truck.

"We need to protect the upstairs as best we can," said Mr. Gabler. "Agustín, can you help me?"

"Yeah, okay sure." Agustín looked at Esther like he would rather spend the time with her, but he followed as Mr. Gabler limped out of the room.

Sasha sat down on the bare side of the bed and crossed her arms. Esther stayed at the window and looked at the orange moon, looming above the neighboring rooftops. She remembered what Agustín had said.

"The moon."

"What?" said Sasha.

"It's been hours, but the moon hasn't moved at all."

"Whatever." Sasha rolled her eyes.

Esther felt some latch she had carefully set in her heart slip, and a lot of feelings came tumbling through her at once. "Of course you don't care. You don't care about anything."

Sasha's mouth went wide in surprise, then snapped tight in fury. "You don't know anything about me. I care about a lot of things. My mom is out on the street right now, defenseless. And you're going to lecture me."

Esther swung around from the window, and she and Sasha faced each other only a few feet apart. "Oh no, your mom is taking a nap in a minivan. My baby sister is missing. Just gone. I have no idea where she is, if she's safe. So excuse me if I'm not too sympathetic that your mom is asleep."

And with that, Sasha started to cry. Big, gulping sobs. Esther had no idea what to do. She was squared off for a fight, and her opponent was wiping tears off her face with the back of her hand.

"Hey," Esther said. "Hey, I didn't mean . . . I'm sure it's scary that your mom . . . You know my parents are also . . . It doesn't matter, we're all scared. It's so scary."

"My little brother," managed Sasha between the sobs that shook her entire body. "Edward. He was in the van. And he's gone. I don't know where he went."

"Your little brother is missing?"

Sasha nodded miserably. Esther sat down on the bed next to her, and wasn't sure what to do next. She put her arm on Sasha's shoulders, and it didn't feel bad at all, so she scooted a little closer, and Sasha put her face into the side of Esther's arm, crying into her. Esther felt hot tears on her arm and started to cry herself.

"My family isn't safe," said Sasha, "and I'm so scared, and I'm stuck here with you and you don't care about me."

"Hey," said Esther, although all of those things had been true until just a moment ago. "No, I care about you."

"Why would you care about me?"

"Because we're human beings. Human beings are supposed to care about each other." Esther hadn't known this to be a fact until that moment, but she felt certain of it as she said it.

"Oh, right," said Sasha. Esther wasn't sure if she was being sarcastic. (Sasha wasn't sure either.)

They were quiet for a long time, except for the occasional sniffle, as the big orange moon placidly shone from precisely the position in the sky where it had been shining since the adults had gone to sleep and the monsters had appeared.

"Why," said Esther, and even as she said it she wasn't sure if it was a good idea, "why are you such a bully to me?"

Sasha pulled away from her. "What?"

"You're always so mean. You're always making fun of me. It sucks. Why do you do that?"

Sasha looked down at her hands, twisted them this way and that. "There are always bullies."

"Yeah, but why do you have to be one of them?"

"I don't know," whispered Sasha. "People say cruel things

about me, and I get so caught up in the anger. And I just want to do what they do to me. I don't even believe the things I say."

"I know," Esther said. "But they're still awful to hear. It's awful to be told that who you are is wrong or inhuman."

"I know. I hear it all the time too."

"It's terrible, being on the wrong side of it."

"It is."

There was another long quiet, but this one felt different. Neither of them was crying anymore. They were caught in something heavy and tangled and vast, and neither of them could see a way out.

"I'm sorry," tried Sasha.

"I don't know if that's enough."

"Okay." Sasha nodded.

"I'm sorry that people are cruel to you too."

"I know." Sasha looked at her. "Are we okay?"

Esther thought about this. "No," she decided. "I don't think that we are. But I think that we could be."

Esther looked solemnly at Sasha, and there was a moment where the conversation could have gone further, and then every remaining window downstairs exploded all at once.

24

ESTHER AND SASHA SCREAMED, an automatic reaction to the sudden noise. After the explosion, there was the soft tinkling of glass settling into itself. Then a heavy footstep, and another, and another. Large feet stomping through the downstairs.

"They're coming!" Agustín called unnecessarily from the hallway.

"What are we going to do?" said Sasha, shutting her eyes under some half belief that if she didn't look at the world for long enough it would leave her alone.

"Okay, we'll . . . ," Esther said, and then realized that she had no idea. She had no more plans, and no more contingencies. Her knowledge mostly extended to horror movies, and none of those offered useful advice in this situation besides filling her head with the most inventively awful things the monsters might do to them.

"Stay in the bedroom, kids," hollered Mr. Gabler. "I'll protect you." And maybe he could. He had before. But Esther didn't think so. Esther didn't think a knife was going to do anything to ward off what would be coming up those stairs. Those creatures were expecting a fight. They were ready for it this time.

Which was when a genuinely useful idea came to Esther. If the creatures were expecting a fight, what if Esther gave them the opposite? What if she could catch the monsters off guard? "Hold on," she shouted, and ran for the bathroom.

"You have to go now?" said Sasha.

Esther ignored her, skidded into the bathroom, and used her entire arm to scoop all of the fake wounds she had left on the counter into her hand. Then she was back in the hallway.

"Can you hold them off?" she asked Mr. Gabler as she sprinted across to the bedroom. He stood on the top landing of the stairs, knife held before him.

"Didn't I tell you to stay in the bedroom? And the answer is yes, very maybe I can possibly hold them off."

"Well, just try to delay them," she said.

"Roger that," he said, in that goofy way adults do when they think they're being funny.

Agustín was already in the bedroom, and he was looking out the window. "There's more of them down there. We can't escape through here."

"I know," said Esther, and then to Sasha: "Lie down."

"What?" Sasha folded her arms again.

"It would take too long to explain, just lie down." Also, Esther didn't want to explain that she would be using Sasha as bait, as she felt that Sasha might not approve of a plan like that. Sasha sighed and lay down, and Esther did her best to stick the wounds to her face.

"Okay," said Esther, "no disrespect to Mr. Gabler, but I think we'll have company soon. And I need your help."

Sasha tried to ask more questions, but with the fake scar pasted across her lips, the most she could manage were a series of inquisitive *mmm*s.

"Yeah, exactly." Esther nodded, in a way that she hoped was reassuring. "You don't have to do anything at all. Just, you know, play dead."

Sasha's eyes went wide.

"No, no," said Esther. "The exact opposite of what you're doing now." Agustín shouted alarm from the doorway while Mr. Gabler hurried in as best he could on an injured ankle. "Okay." She patted Sasha reassuringly. "Keep real still, and we'll all be fine."

Then she grabbed the others and pulled them down behind the bed. There was a moment of silence. Esther hoped Sasha would be able to play her part.

The door creaked open. A wheezing laugh, and behind it a disharmonic chorus of clicks and buzzes. The shuffle of footsteps.

Esther had assumed that whatever these creatures were in their trick-or-treat costumes, they would be expecting a last stand from their targets. They had prepared for a fight.

And so she had presented them with the opposite of what they were prepared for. No one in sight, except one girl on the floor, lying limp and still, covered in wounds. There would, Esther hoped, be confusion. And in that confusion lived their only chance to escape.

She dared a glance around the bed. Sure enough, the three trick-or-treaters were bunched up by the door, apparently unsure of what to do. Finally they shambled forward, fanning out through the room. The clown slumped down to check on Sasha.

Don't move, Sasha, thought Esther. *Please don't move.* And although she did not believe in telepathy, she could feel Sasha respond: *I hate you so much, Esther Gold.*

But Esther had no intention of leaving Sasha defenseless for long. As soon as the other trick-or-treaters moved away from the door, she bellowed, "GO!" and started running without looking back to see if the other two were following. As she went, she scooped Sasha up to standing with one arm. Sasha was light, and she came up stumbling.

"I've got you," Esther said.

"I hate you so much, Esth—"

"Yeah, yeah, I know."

Unprepared for this series of events, the trick-or-treaters did nothing to stop the four of them from tearing out of the room, down the stairs, and through the still-open front door. She could hear Mr. Gabler grunting each time his weight shifted to his right foot, but he managed to keep up all the same.

They made it as far as Mr. Nathaniel's immaculate driveway next door before Dan's apple truck roared in reverse up the lawn and blocked their escape. They turned to go the other way, and there was Ed's truck, churning up the grass as it cut them off. Now the only way was down the driveway and into the street, and so they started for it.

Esther came tripping to a stop, along with the others, when an obstacle she absolutely did not anticipate appeared before her.

The woman who had stepped out into the driveway was wearing a purple gown, with trims of green and accents of glittering jewels. These reflected the streetlights and the giant orange moon in a scattered gleaming. But more than light, the woman radiated power. She looked as though not a single person had ever said no to her, not once in a thousand years. (This impression was, more or less, accurate.)

In her hands she cradled, as though it were a fragile and beloved child, a small black box locked with a complex silver clasp.

Esther felt the turkey she had eaten in Mr. Gabler's kitchen start to return on her as she realized she recognized the woman. The woman had been floating in the park outside of school that morning, however many hours ago that morning had been.

"So," the woman said, in a voice as expensive and gaudy as her jewelry, "you're the ones causing a fuss." She scrunched her nose. "I thought you'd be taller."

"Who are you?" whispered Esther.

"Yeah," said Agustín a little louder. "Who are you?"

"Ah," the woman said to Esther, with a laugh that sounded like coins thrown in a fountain. "You have your own lackeys. Good for you."

"Hey!" said Agustín.

"Hey!" said Mr. Gabler.

Behind their queen, the buzzing and clicking trick-or-treaters gathered. Mr. Gabler clutched his knife, but the creatures made no move to approach. Instead, they were lowering themselves onto whatever part of their body was similar to a knee. On either side, Dan and Ed were also kneeling, heads bowed.

"Hello," said the woman. "I am pleased to make all of your acquaintances, however brief that acquaintance will be. I"—she put one regal hand upon her regal chest—"am the Queen of Halloween."

25

"I KNOW WHAT YOU'RE THINKING. You didn't even know that Halloween had a queen. But children, and here I include you, Mr. Dentist. Mr. Dentist, I'm unclear how you managed to stay awake, but I'm sure the answer is utterly uninteresting. Children, you understand so little about this holiday. For you it is a time to dress up and gorge yourself on catastrophic amounts of sugar. For me, it is my territory, my domain, that I can rule and alter and destroy as I see fit.

"Now, you were given a chance, weren't you? To go to sleep like the others? It's nice in the Dream. In the Dream, nothing hurts, and nothing matters, because nothing is real. Out here everything is real, and so everything hurts very much indeed. Here the treats are loaded with blades and the decorations explode and the costumes are tattered and hold horrible creatures within. And none of this has to be yours to confront. All you would need to do is close your eyes and dream.

"Ah, but why speak of regret? What should have been. What could have been. Ugh. A sad business, and not worth our time. Instead, let's talk of what's going to be. So much more hopeful, the future.

"Not that the future exists, per se, at the moment. Time doesn't so much exist. It's Halloween night, and as long as that Halloween moon shines in the sky, it will continue to be Halloween night. I'm sure you've felt it. It has been Halloween night for far too many hours already, yes? And it will be Halloween night for many hours more. Many days more. Months. Years.

"Time doesn't work that way, I know. But that was in your world. And you're not in your world anymore, not exactly. Once the sun set, you and everyone in this neighborhood crossed the borders into a wild country, one in which lives everything you've ever been afraid of. And I am its queen. So it will be Halloween night, and the adults will sleep, and my creatures will creep forever. Because that's what I want.

"And I always, always, always get what I want."

As she spoke, she stepped closer and closer up the driveway, and Esther and the rest stepped back and back, until they had run into Mr. Nathaniel's garage door and there was nowhere else to retreat. Now this strange woman was only a few feet away, and she held out one hand, in invitation or threat, Esther wasn't sure. She wouldn't find out, because the queen was interrupted by the sound of a hose turning on, followed by a gushing of cold water.

"No, no, no." The queen coughed with a guttural fear that confused Esther. The self-proclaimed monarch, now dripping wet, retreated back down the driveway, putting the little black box behind her back to better protect it.

There at the top of the walk was Mr. Nathaniel, with his hose.

"Hey!" he shouted, spraying again. Dan and Ed and the trick-or-treaters all scrambled to avoid the water. "Get!"

"Thank you, Mr. Nathaniel," said Esther.

"Mmm," he grunted, not taking his narrowed eyes off the woman at the bottom of the drive.

"Yes, thanks, Charlie," said Mr. Gabler, using a name that Esther had not known until now. "I know this must all seem so unbelievable, but you see those costumed children down there don't seem to be children at all, and—"

"Shut up," said Mr. Nathaniel.

"Excuse me?" said Mr. Gabler.

"That's right," said the Queen of Halloween, trying to regain some of the dignity of her posture. She brought her voice back up to a commanding register. "Be quiet, all of you, for you are in the presence of—"

"Shut up," repeated Mr. Nathaniel, and wheeled the spray of water in her direction. She yelped and scrambled backward.

Now everyone was quiet. Mr. Nathaniel put one hand on his hip.

"All of you out here on this night, making all kinds of ruckus. I hate ruckus. I hate this night."

"Well of course *you* would," said Dan, and then he immediately cowered back behind his truck as Mr. Nathaniel flicked his eyes toward him.

"I didn't know you were here," said the queen. "I would have chosen another . . . but it's too late now. Just, you stay out of my way and I'll stay out of yours."

"You know Mr. Nathaniel?" Esther asked her.

"Mr. Nathaniel." The queen laughed. "I know this man, but not by that absurd little name." She flicked her head derisively at Mr. Nathaniel. "Really, is that the kind of title you chose for yourself?"

"I don't need to explain myself to you," said the old man.

"Charlie," said Mr. Gabler. "Do you know these creatures? What is going on?"

"I don't need to explain myself to anyone," said Mr. Nathaniel. "I moved to this neighborhood for peace and quiet, and by god that's what I'll have."

He marched down the driveway, the denizens of Halloween moving away from him to keep out of range of the hose.

"So you all"—he shouted at the queen and her minions—"you all will move on and leave these people alone."

"That's right, get out of here," said Agustín.

"And you," said Mr. Nathaniel, wheeling on the small group standing in his driveway. "You aren't nearly afraid enough, so you must not know anything at all. Because anyone who understood what was happening here would get as far away from it as possible. I suggest you run."

"What is happening?" said Esther. "Please, if you know, tell us."

"Isn't it obvious? Have you seen that moon move even a little, in hours and hours? Now I said run." Mr. Nathaniel made one last spray with his hose for emphasis, the vapor drifting by them, chilly in the fall night air.

So they ran. They ran down the driveway and then down the street. Dan and Ed and their queen and the mysterious trick-or-treaters made no move to stop them. All seemed paralyzed in fear of Mr. Nathaniel, whoever he actually was.

As they ran, Esther puzzled over one detail. The vapor from the hose hadn't tasted like tap water. The water was salty and full of minerals and a little bit alive. It wasn't tap water. It was seawater.

26

"WHO WAS THAT WOMAN?" SAID AGUSTÍN.

"I have no idea. And I have no idea why they all seem to know Mr. Nathaniel or why they're all afraid of him," Esther said.

"Well, Charlie is a little scary, I guess," said Mr. Gabler.

"Let's just keep moving," said Sasha, glancing back.

"I want to check on my mother," said Agustín.

"Of course," said Esther. She hated that she hadn't suggested it first, that he had had to remind her that he also was scared because this situation was, objectively, scary.

They moved as quickly as Mr. Gabler was able, keeping an eye out for anyone following them, but no one did. Passing by the canyon, the high school party there seemed to have grown. Lights and voices, celebrating, barbarous and remote from the considerations of the town around them.

Something about the party made Esther shudder.

But she soon forgot the high schoolers' party as they approached Agustín's block and saw something truly extraordinary.

Agustín's house was easy to spot, even from a distance, because it had transformed completely. Where once had been a modest plot with a few sample grave markers in the front yard, now there was a massive cemetery with tall black fences. The gate to the cemetery was chained shut. The gravestones were ancient black monoliths, several stories tall. The writing on them was in glyphs that did not look like any language Esther knew. Badly maintained paths wound their way through the overgrown cemetery as it sloped up a steep hill. More and more vines appeared among the other plants, until the hillside became choked with vines in its upper slopes, steep cliffs that were more vine than rock. And at the summit, Agustín's mother's workshop, perched atop the vine-shrouded hill. The light in the workshop was on, and even from that distance they could see the shadow of his mother, moving back and forth. Somehow, they could also hear her, humming and hammering away, hard at work and seemingly oblivious to the inexplicable transformation of her yard.

"Mom!" shouted Agustín. "Mom, can you hear me?" But there was no response. His voice echoed out through the gravestones, until it was absorbed by the choking vines that covered the hill.

He rattled the locked gate. "What is happening?"

"I don't know," said Esther, because how could she? Nothing she had thought she had known about the world would explain what was happening here. "But I do know we need help."

"Maybe we should go to the police," said Sasha. "I know 9-1-1 isn't working, but we could walk to the station."

"No," said Agustín and Esther.

"No!" said Mr. Gabler with a vehemence that surprised them all.

"Okay, it was just a suggestion." Sasha threw up her hands. "You all are so mean."

"I've got to try to climb up there," said Agustín, touching the fence experimentally.

"I know from climbing," Mr. Gabler said. "And I don't see a way. Even for me."

"We could go to the hospital," said Esther.

"None of us are sick," said Agustín.

"I know. But Mr. Gabler hurt his ankle. Maybe they could help. And anyway, it feels like as safe a place as possible."

"Okay," said Mr. Gabler, clapping his hands. "We need a destination, and the hospital is as good as any."

Agustín stood undecided, looking up at the silhouette of his mother, unreachably high in her curious perch. He sighed. "She's probably happier this way. Finally left alone with her work." Esther tried to touch his arm, but he turned away and started walking. "Let's go to the hospital."

The hospital was many miles down the hill from their neighborhood, on the other side of the dry riverbed.

"Mr. Gabler?" Esther said.

He was insisting on walking quickly, his face drawn tight with the pain. As he walked, he tossed something back and forth in his palms. It was the small, sharp stone that had woken him up at the start of this strange night. He smiled a little when he saw her looking, and held it up for her to see.

"A souvenir from a different me, a long time ago," he said. "I haven't thought about this in years." He looked down at it and smiled. "But I suppose it did us all a big favor by waking me up tonight." He put it back in his pocket and patted the pocket fondly. "There was something you wanted to talk to me about?"

"Where did you learn how to climb up the outside of a house?"

"I wasn't always—"

"A dentist, I know, but what does that mean?"

Mr. Gabler didn't say anything for so long that Esther started to think he was ignoring the question. She had so utterly misjudged the kind of person he was, and she wanted to understand how that had happened. She was wrestling with whether to leave him to his privacy or to push again when he finally responded.

"I used to have a job that I shouldn't have had. I didn't like having that job, and I regret having it."

"Was it illegal?"

He shrugged in a way that meant yes.

"Oh my god, did you steal things?"

"Yes, Esther, I stole things. I worked for a man, a bad man

who paid me to steal for him. But it's funny how life works."

"How's that?"

"The man I worked for got robbed himself and sent to jail just this month. I had tried not to think of him for so long. And then when I saw that article about his 'museum,' well, it was certainly a shock."

Esther was wrestling with all of the implications of this news when a tiny creature ran out into the street in front of them.

"Ugh," said Sasha. "A black cat. Shoo!" She waved her arms.

"No," said Esther. "There's nothing wrong with black cats. We only think badly of them because some awful person made up lies about them."

She knelt and held out her hand. The black cat looked back at her with golden eyes, seeming to take judgment of Esther's every deed and misdeed, and at last, finding her worthy, it took a few steps forward and nuzzled her hand.

"Good kitty."

"It *is* cute," said Agustín, joining Esther in petting it.

"Okay, yes, I guess it's cute," admitted Sasha, watching while pretending she wasn't.

The cat purred at them and then cocked its head. Its ears twitched, and it dashed into the bushes at the side of the road.

"I don't know what it heard," said Mr. Gabler. "But I respect its instincts. Let's get out of here."

"Bye, kitty," Esther called behind them as they left.

* * *

What felt like hours passed and still they walked. The geography of the streets was off. Each block was longer than it'd been in the daylight. Some of the cul-de-sacs looked unfamiliar, full of old houses Esther had never seen before, teetering wooden structures that wouldn't last through a single one of California's earthquakes.

"Man, this walk is tiring, right?" Esther said to Sasha.

"I'm not a weakling. You don't have to worry about me. Worry about yourself."

Esther felt a biting comeback in her mouth. It tasted like sour candy and felt like thumbtacks. She let it dissipate. Instead, she said, "Sorry. I'm just tired. That's all I meant."

Sasha kicked at a loose piece of asphalt. "I'm sorry too. I don't mean to be so defensive. But people have assumed I'm weak my whole life. So I just . . ."

"I get it."

Sasha and Esther looked at each other, and Esther almost smiled, but instead she turned back ahead and continued into the night.

Every once in a while, one of the brothers' trucks drove by, and they would all jump down behind a fence or a wall to hide. The trucks drove slowly, and Ed and Dan both kept their windows down, staring out at their surroundings as if they had X-ray vision. Esther knew exactly who those two were looking for.

At other times, Esther swore she saw bizarre shapes moving on distant blocks. Gamboling creatures that did not look like any animal she knew. Silhouettes that did not look like any kind of human at all. She had the strong feeling that this endless night did not belong to people. She shuddered to think what else waited for them before the moon finally set.

"I should have tried to climb the gate," said Agustín, startling her after they had walked in silence for the better part of an hour.

"Huh?" she said.

"Where my mom is. I should have tried to hop the fence. I should have tried to climb that hill. Even if it was impossible, I should have tried."

"We're all doing the best we can," said Esther. She reached out to take his hand, then stopped, suddenly nervous to do so. She dropped her hand back at her side. "You did the best you could."

"Maybe." He wouldn't meet her eye. "But she works so hard for me, you know? I could have worked a little harder for her. I get so frustrated about how much she works, and I shouldn't. I know I shouldn't. It's my fault she works like that, and I didn't even try to save her."

"Hey." She touched his arm. "If I thought you should have done more, do you think I would lie to you and tell you otherwise?"

He seemed to genuinely consider the question.

"No, Esther Gold. I don't think you would lie to me."

They continued on in silence, but he no longer looked behind them. Instead, Esther did.

Even from this distance, she could still see the hill,

knotted with vines, and the workshop teetering at the top, and the light in the window, and somehow also the woman in the light, and even miles away by some cruel miracle she could still hear Agustín's mother humming through the long, long night.

MARKING OF EXACT TIME was nearly impossible. Nothing in the sky had moved, and while their phones and Mr. Gabler's watch continued to show times, the progress of the numbers was erratic, sometimes forward, sometimes backward, and so was not useful in measuring anything but the strangeness of the night.

Still, the ache in their feet provided a clear sense of the distance they had traveled and how long it had taken to travel it.

"I don't think I've walked this long in forever," Agustín said.

Sasha thought about it. "You know, I genuinely don't think I've ever walked this long," she said. "My mom never likes me to walk."

Only Mr. Gabler didn't seem that tired. "Lots of running,"

he explained. "How else am I supposed to maintain this?" He patted his paunch. "Careful daily training." He laughed. But he was favoring his left leg more and more, and Esther could tell that the pain was getting to him.

Esther was exhausted and sore, but she didn't want to show it. She wanted to be the one urging them on, moving them toward some kind of resolution.

"It hasn't been that long," she said. "And we're almost there. See? There's the bridge."

Just before the administrative parking lot that connected to both the hospital and police station was the bridge across Calleguas Creek. Calleguas Creek was not a creek, but a broad riverbed, sandy with the occasional cluster of trees. For almost the entire year it was dry, and used by locals as a place to walk dogs, hold paint gun fights, and sneak to teenage hiding places in the trees. But on the few weeks a year that it rained, it would fill, startlingly quickly, with shallow but fast-moving water. The rise of the water could be frighteningly violent.

Every kid in town had been taught to stay well away from the creek when the weather was wet, or even if it had snowed recently in the distant mountains, since the snowmelt could cause a wave of water to rush through the riverbed with little warning. They were shown videos in class and told stories of people being swept away in water like that. Only eight inches of water at that velocity was enough to knock over and carry off a full-grown adult, they were told.

Once, Esther and Agustín had been wandering around the canyon during the dry part of the year. (Most of the year was the dry part of the year.) There was a large property owned by the Catholic church next to the river, and the property had a tall drainage tunnel leading directly into the riverbed. Often, they would climb up to it, walk through, and wander the property until some priest or other church employee caught them and ushered them irritably back out to the street.

On this particular day, they had recently been taught about the dangers of the water and so were jumpy despite knowing that no precipitation had fallen anywhere in Southern California for weeks. Still, there wasn't much to do in a town like theirs, so they'd walked down into Calleguas Creek and headed for the drain tunnel. Just as they got to it and were preparing to climb up, they heard the unmistakable hiss of water.

She and Agustín had looked at each other with wide, panicked eyes. And then water had started pouring from the drainpipe. Neither of them had ever run so fast in their lives, both of them thinking about the lesson that had basically told them that a single toe dipped into water in that riverbed could be death in the fast-moving current. They hadn't stopped running when they got back to the street, running all the way to Agustín's house and collapsing on his lawn, feeling the dry bristling grass beneath them with relief.

Now, a couple years later, she thought about the meager stream of water coming from the drain and understood that it had only been a groundskeeper hosing out the tunnel. But in the moment, that panic had been absolute and real. Tonight they were in a situation in which the menace was truly dangerous, and she felt much calmer. A person's level of fear, she realized, is often totally unrelated to their actual level of danger.

The group approached the bridge. It hadn't rained for several weeks, so there was a sense of wrongness and unease that swept through them when they heard a roar that sounded very much like a river.

"Maybe it snowed in the mountains," Mr. Gabler said.

"Maybe," Esther said, not believing it. They stepped out onto the bridge and looked over the side.

"Whoa," Agustín said.

"That's impossible," Sasha said.

None of them had ever seen the river like that. Even at its highest points, Calleguas Creek was always only a few feet deep, and it rarely even spread across the entire sandy riverbed. But the river below them climbed almost all the way to the bridge. It looked like a river out of the rain forest. Water that belonged to a wet, green world, nothing like the climate they lived in. The mist from the rapids below made their clothes damp.

"What could have caused this?" Esther said. They looked at Mr. Gabler, hoping the only adult would have the answers. He raised his hands.

"I have no idea. Adults know less than you'd think. We certainly don't know anything about this."

"There's something on the river," Agustín said.

Sure enough, there were boats coming down the river. Esther and the rest realized one by one that they were actually huge tree trunks, taller and broader than any tree that grew in this part of the world. Riding on the trunks were figures in red waterproof jumpsuits, yellow boots, and red hats pulled low over their faces. The figures balanced impossibly on the trees, as easily as a tourist strolling on the deck of a cruise ship.

One of the figures looked up. He was a middle-aged man, younger than Esther's parents but older than any of her cousins. He had stubble and a crooked nose, but mostly what he had was one eye. One big eye in the middle of his face above his nose. He met her eyes with his eye until his tree had passed under the bridge and he was gone.

No one said anything.

"Okay," Esther said. She thought of all of the things they could talk about, but the sooner they moved forward, the better. She waved her hand in front of her as though to indicate all that she wasn't saying. "Let's just get to the hospital."

The rest of them looked at each other and saw that none of them wanted to discuss what they had seen, so they all kept walking.

Their destination wasn't far now. They could see the tower of the hospital building, lights in the windows, signs of what could be normal human activity. In front of the tower was a thick bank of fog, unusual but not impossible for the climate. They stepped into the murk.

The fog was absolute. They could see only a few feet in front of them, and so had no choice but to follow the curve of the sidewalk. The hospital was right down the street. As long as they didn't accidentally turn off the main road, they would be fine, and even with the fog that didn't seem likely.

So they were all surprised when they ran into a tree. Literally, in Esther's case.

"Ow. Man. What is a tree doing here?"

There had always been trees along the roads, planted by the city, but those had been wispy, water-starved things. This was a healthy giant, the same size as the tree trunks they had seen on the river, the ones that none of them were talking about.

"This doesn't seem right. Is this right? It doesn't seem like it," Sasha said.

"Maybe we walked off the road?" Agustín suggested. But there was still sidewalk under their feet. The asphalt of the street was visible to their right. There was just a huge tree none of them had seen before in the middle of the sidewalk.

"We're almost to the hospital," Mr. Gabler said. "We can figure all this out when we get there."

They went around the tree and picked their way through the fog. Soon there were more giant trees, and they had to be careful not to repeat Esther's collision.

"This isn't right," Agustín said. "We're definitely off the road."

"No, look, we're still on the sidewalk," Esther said. And they were. Just a sidewalk next to an asphalt road. But they were also standing on a forest floor, dense with rotting leaves and moss. Both of these facts were true at the same time, even though they definitely couldn't be. She stared at her feet, seeing both realities at once.

"Change of plan," she said. "Gus was right, we've gotten off the road somehow. Let's backtrack."

They tried to, but every direction looked the same, and now there were no signs of manmade surfaces, only the forest floor and the trees. They were in the middle of thick woods, but there were no thick woods in this town, Esther thought. Only backyard lawns and community pools and orange groves.

As if in response to that thought, she saw a tree ahead with big orange fruit. Okay, now she knew where they were. They had stumbled somehow into an orange grove. Never mind that the nearest orange grove was well up the hill from the bridge, never mind that the forest they were walking through looked nothing like an orange grove, there was an orange tree in front of them, so: orange grove.

The fog dissipated a bit, and they saw the tree clearly, and all of Esther's justifications failed her.

It was another tree, like the others, but this one had branches hanging low and heavy with round orange fruit. Not oranges. The fruit hanging from the branches were jack-o'-lanterns, each one a unique carved face, each one lit from within with a single candle. When the wind blew, the tree creaked and the jack-o'-lanterns danced, the flames inside them flickering. It was beautiful. It was wrong. It scared Esther deeply. She gaped at it, frozen by the fearful unnaturalness of it.

She heard the soft mew of a cat.

At the foot of the jack-o'-lantern tree, sitting with its tail wrapped neatly around its body, was the little black cat they had seen earlier.

"Hey there, kitty," Esther said. "Do you know what's going on? Because we don't."

The cat mewed again, and then it turned and walked into the fog. They looked at each other. Mr. Gabler shrugged, and they all followed it.

28

THE CAT WAS STARK BLACK against the white sheet of fog, but even still, it was small and quick, and they had to hurry to keep up. They stumbled over roots, bumped against trees that loomed suddenly into visibility inches away from unprotected faces. Every once in a while, the cat would pause to let them catch up, and then dart away again.

"How did this go from a trip to the hospital to following a cat through a magic forest?" Mr. Gabler asked.

"That's a question a lot of people ask themselves when they get to be your age," Agustín said.

Mr. Gabler grinned despite himself. Then he tripped on a pile of slippery leaves and landed butt first in the dirt, howling in pain as the impact jarred his ankle.

"Alright, I've had it," he said. "This was a bad plan. I don't want to follow a cat anymore."

"Doesn't look like we have a choice," Esther said. The cat was gone. They were alone in the silent, foggy woods. Off in the gloom in front of them, eerie lights flickered.

"Come on. I guess let's head toward the mysterious lights," she said.

"Sure," Agustín said, "that's never a sentence that has turned out badly." But he followed her as she marched into the mist.

The lights resolved into the most peculiar house Esther had ever seen. Some of it looked like a medieval villager's hut out of a movie. Straw thatching. Mud walls. A well outside with a rope and bucket system. But the windows were modern, double-paned, well insulated. There was a modern stucco chimney sticking out of the thatched roof. A satellite dish was tucked into the thatching. There was a modern mailbox a few yards from the front door.

"What in the world?" muttered Mr. Gabler.

"I don't think this is our world," said Esther.

"Guys?" Sasha said, pointing.

A woman had emerged from the front door, which was modern and painted bright red. She was wearing a black wool robe and had gray hair, although she didn't seem much older than Mr. Gabler.

"Welcome," the woman said. "My name is Aileen. Come on inside." She gave a beckoning wave and shuffled back into the bizarre house.

"Couldn't be any weirder than outside," Agustín said, and headed in. Esther shrugged and followed. Sasha and

Mr. Gabler hurried after.

"I have a stew going," the woman said, once they were inside. There was a fire pit with a huge open fire. Hanging from a thick hook over the fire was a black metal pot, full of bubbling thick stew. "It's not going to be ready for a bit, I'm afraid. Let me microwave up a pizza."

The interior was as baffling as its exterior. The floor of the hut was dirt. About half of the walls were the same mud as the outside. The other half had floral-print wallpaper and a few electrical outlets. Tucked around the fire were rough straw mattresses, with modern sheets and pillows on them. Near the fire pit was a fridge, and a sink, and a microwave. The woman pulled a pizza out of the freezer and popped it into the microwave.

"I know, I know," she said, "you're supposed to bake these, but it's a little hard to do that on an open fire. Comes out too crispy. Also pretty ashy." The woman gestured around the house and its jumble of ancient and new. "As you can see, things aren't so linear around here."

"Where is here?" Esther said.

"You," Aileen said, "are in a Dream."

"We're dreaming?" Sasha said.

"No. You are completely awake. You are in the Dream of Halloween."

Mr. Gabler sat down on one of the straw mattresses. He folded his hands in his lap. "It really has been a weird night."

"I agree to go trick-or-treating once, and I end up stuck

in my least favorite holiday," muttered Agustín.

The microwave beeped, and the woman pulled out a steaming pizza, setting it on the rough wooden table. Esther realized it had been a long time since she had eaten, and the sight of the food made all of that hunger come back to her. They all grabbed slices, stuffing them almost whole into their mouths.

"Hungry lot," Aileen said. "Look, I know it's confusing. It's because you're not supposed to be here. A human crossing over like this isn't something that is ever supposed to happen."

The woman sat on a stool by the table and watched them eat.

"Here's my best explanation," she said. "The Dream of Halloween is its own world. Lived here my whole life. Lovely place. Cheap real estate. You wouldn't believe what I got this property for. Fifteen hundred square feet, and it only cost two years of my laughter. Of course, those two years weren't a picnic. Couldn't watch comedies. It didn't hurt when I tried to laugh. Just nothing happened and it spooked me good. Sorry, besides the point. Now, the Dream is connected to your world in a number of ways. Sleep, obviously. We're tied pretty closely to how you sleep. But there is also a holiday you people set up to honor our connection."

"Labor Day," Agustín said.

"Funny kid," Aileen said. "I don't like funny kids. They remind me of the two years I couldn't laugh. Anyway, during Halloween our worlds get close together. Sometimes they even touch."

"Is that how we ended up here?" Esther asked.

"Maybe." The woman frowned. "Under ordinary circumstances it should have been impossible for you to get here without knowing it exists. But it appears circumstances aren't ordinary tonight. Someone very high up must have done something very wrong." She looked out the window, as though making sure they weren't being watched. "These days that could only mean the queen."

"The queen," Esther said. "We saw a queen. We think. Mr. Nathaniel said she stopped time, but he wouldn't tell us anything else."

Aileen got up from her stool and paced by the fire.

"No," she said. "That's not something our queen can do. That's far beyond her capabilities. No one could have done that except maybe—no, he wouldn't. And anyway, he's long gone."

She stopped pacing and spoke quite urgently. Esther tried to look as studious and attentive as she could, given that she had a glob of cheese hanging off her lip and sauce smeared on her cheeks.

"Living in the Dream of Halloween has its drawbacks," Aileen said. "It's a powerful place, and bad people tend to get drawn to powerful places. We've had a number of evil and corrupt rulers, going back to our first one. But our current queen is . . . well, she's no worse than the rest, I suppose. Which is to say she's pretty terrible."

"If she's the one we've met, then she's not very pleasant, no," Mr. Gabler said, from his place on the floor. He was the only one who hadn't gone for the pizza. He looked tired and worried. Esther remembered that his wife was lying in their bed at home, asleep, like everyone else was asleep. Unwakeable.

"She's very powerful, our queen," the woman said. "But her power is tied to a lot of things beyond her control. For instance, the closer your world gets to Halloween, the more her power grows. Then it wanes again as the year moves away from Halloween.

"But even more than the holiday, her power is tied to the moon," she continued. "When there is a full moon on Halloween, which only happens once every couple of decades, that is when she is most powerful. It's a dangerous time for anyone else to be out. Most citizens of the Dream of Halloween are locked tight in their houses tonight."

"So that would explain why she would want to freeze time," Esther said. "If this is when she is most powerful, and she froze time tonight . . ."

"Then she would stay that powerful forever, yes, in theory," Aileen said. "But even the queen isn't powerful enough to stop time. The source of her power is itself the movement of time. It would be like trying to stop a waterwheel with more water. It's impossible."

"I think I've heard enough about things being impossible for tonight," Mr. Gabler said, lying back and putting his fingers on his temples. "None of it is impossible if it has already happened."

"'Sa good point," Agustín managed through a big bite of pizza. Sasha had her mouth full as well, but she nodded.

"Not impossible then," Aileen said. "But she couldn't have done it alone. She must have found someone, or something, that gave her more power than she would have on her own."

"What kind of thing could do that?" asked Esther.

"I genuinely have no idea." Aileen shook her head. "If she truly has gained power, then that is terrible news for us all."

She took the empty pizza box and tossed it into a plastic garbage bin.

"You were all so hungry," she said. "I would guess you are also quite tired. You can sleep. You'll be safe here from whatever is affecting your neighborhood. We'll talk more when you're rested."

Esther was about to protest and then realized that the woman was right. She was exhausted to the core.

"Grab any mattress," Aileen said. "Bathroom's through there if you'd like to wash up. Although I'm afraid I should warn you that the toilet is one of the medieval parts of the house."

Agustín opened the door she indicated. He made a face and closed it again.

"I think I can hold it," he said, and lay down on one of the mattresses.

ESTHER WOKE UP TO the smell of pancakes. The woman in the black robe was pouring batter into a cast-iron pan on a grate over the fire.

"Thought you might like breakfast, even if it's not really morning," she said.

"Breakfast?" Agustín said, already rolling off the mattress. Esther sat up, her back stiff. She hadn't slept well. Straw mattresses were, as it turns out, not comfortable.

"Glad you're all awake," Aileen said, banging the pan around to make sure they were all definitely awake. "I've been sitting up this whole time. Trying to figure it out." She nodded at the window. "Should be morning by now, but it's still the same foggy night. Seems you're right. She's frozen time, both in your world and in our Dream. I thought I knew everything she could do, but I guess I was wrong."

She tapped her fingers nervously on her hip. "We could all be in a great deal of danger."

"You seem to know a lot about her," Esther said. She didn't mean it suspiciously, necessarily, but she didn't mean it not suspiciously either.

Aileen nodded. "I know the queen very, very well," she said. She didn't elaborate, just put the pancakes on plates and passed them out to her hungry guests.

Mr. Gabler stretched his ankle experimentally. "Seems better," he said. "I think sleep helped."

"Here," Esther said, handing a plate to Sasha.

"Thanks," Sasha mumbled, without meeting her eyes.

"Now," Aileen continued, "given what's happened, I think at least one mystery's been solved. I know how you got into the Dream."

"Lay it on us, Columbo," Mr. Gabler said. Esther, Agustín, and Sasha stared at him blankly. "Columbo?" he said. "Guy on TV? Detective? No? God, I'm old." He glumly took a bite of pancake.

"The queen," Aileen said, ignoring the dejected dentist, "has created a small bubble of frozen time in your world. She couldn't stop time for an entire universe, or even an entire planet. Even with whatever new power she has gained, there simply is no way that any creature could manage that. So she froze time in one single small place. Your neighborhood."

"Great, another reason living in our town sucks," Sasha said.

"With that much power in such a small place," Aileen continued, apparently having decided to ignore the frequent interruptions and plow through her explanation, "the two worlds have been drawn closer together. The boundary between them is gossamer thin, especially at the edges of the bubble. You approached that edge and began to see elements of the Dream poking through into your reality."

"The river," Agustín said. "With the cyclops guys and the logs."

"Oh, you saw the Loggers of the Screaming Woods? Huh, they might have helped you if you could have communicated to them what was going on. But then, I'm not sure you would have liked the way they communicate." She grimaced. "Their language is based on smell rather than sound. Oh well. Doesn't matter. As you poked at the edge of the bubble of frozen time, you accidentally slipped through into the Dream, and then made your way to this house."

"A cat led us," Esther said. "A black cat."

"I doubt that," the woman said, frowning.

"It did!" Esther felt herself go red.

"Mmm," the woman said. She tucked her hands into the sleeves of her robe. "In any case, it's lucky you found me. There are dangerous things in the Dream. Dangerous even for me, let alone some humans who have never been here before. Not all of the Dream is as cozy as this."

They looked around at the mud walls and the door to the toilet they had avoided using, to their great discomfort.

"But she didn't just stop time," Sasha said. "She also put everyone to sleep."

"If she didn't need the people for her plan, she could have pushed them into the Dream to get them out of the way. Putting them to sleep would have been the easiest way to do that."

"So they're somewhere around here?" Esther said hopefully.

"No, the Dream is not one continuous place. It has been fought over so many times by so many different powerful rulers that it has been shattered into pieces. Not all the pieces are as . . . logical as this. She could have simply pushed them into some isolated fragment of the Dream, one with no entrance or exit except the one she created and then locked shut. To the people, your friends and your family, it would feel like they were asleep and dreaming, except, of course, it would never end."

"I've got to rescue my mom," said Agustín. "I'm not just going to leave her up there. She would do anything to rescue me if I were trapped."

"And what about the children?" Esther said. "They took my sister and Sasha's—"

"They took my brother, and I want him back," Sasha said. "I don't even really like him, but I don't want him kidnapped by the queen."

Aileen looked sharply at her. "She has taken children again? That is . . . well it's not good."

"Oh, it's not?" Esther said, trying to put as much sarcasm into the three words as she possibly could.

"Scholars in the Dream have never been able to verify this, but there are stories that the queen has an army of children. Children that she captured from your world and took to the Dream with her. Children she raised, acting as a kind of mother. Trust me, you don't want the queen as your mother. Having spent so long in the Dream of Halloween, they lost their humanity and turned into beings of pure Dream, held together by her power, keeping only the vestiges of the children they once were."

"I think . . . I think we saw some of those," Esther said, remembering with a shudder trick-or-treaters buzzing and clicking like insects. "Is that what she's doing to Sharon?"

"Impossible to say for sure," Aileen said. "Certainly she hasn't had time to do anything yet."

"We need to get them back right now," Sasha said.

Aileen bit her lip. "I'm not sure that's possible."

"How do we go back?" Mr. Gabler said.

"If your town is still touching the Dream, then you should be able to just walk from one world to the other if you know where to go. Follow me."

She led them out of her house and around to the back. Behind her house the woods sloped down into a steep hill. There was a stone staircase leading down the hill.

"These stairs will take you to the edge of this fragment of the Dream. Once you reach that edge, you will go . . . somewhere else. My hope is it will be somewhere back in your neighborhood."

"Your hope?" Esther said.

"Dreams are unpredictable. They don't work by the rules of your world. Good luck, Esther Gold."

"I never told you my name."

"No, you did not."

"How do you know so much about the queen?"

Aileen crouched down and whispered to her.

"The queen is a cruel and terrible ruler. There was a resistance against her in the Dream. We fought her for years. We spied on her, sabotaged her, worked at every turn to bring her down. We were known as the Black Cats."

"But there was a black cat . . . ," Esther said.

"The queen hated us. She started quite a lot of rumors and superstitions about black cats, in an attempt to eradicate us from both the Dream and your world. And it worked. Our revolution failed. I hid here, in this quiet corner of the Dream. If the queen truly has gained power, it is time for you to flee, and for you to hide. If you keep poking at the edges of the bubble, you might be able to find your way back to the rest of your world."

"We can't do that," Esther said uncertainly.

"If you face the queen, she will beat you. She will win. Run away, Esther Gold."

Esther tilted her head, looked into Aileen's eyes, trying to find something there, unsure what she was even looking for.

"You were the black cat. You were the little cat that led us through the woods to your house."

Aileen smiled.

"That seems like a ridiculous idea."

"But it's true, isn't it?"

"I doubt it. Esther Gold, it was good to meet you." The

woman held out her hand. She had long and sharp nails. Esther gripped carefully around them to shake her hand. "I am Aileen, leader of the Black Cats. Please remember what I said. It's not too late for you to get away."

"Thank you for your help," Esther said. She turned, and the four of them started carefully picking their way down the steps. After a few steps she looked back, but Aileen wasn't there. Esther thought she could hear the patter of tiny feet running away, but it didn't seem all that likely.

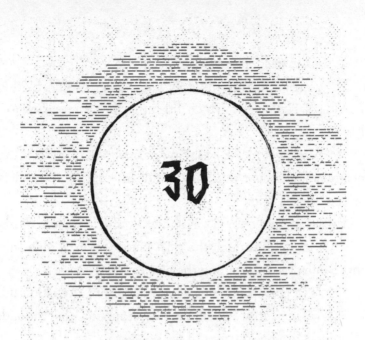

THE STAIRS LED DOWN AND DOWN, along the gentle slope of a hillside, which gradually became a steep slope with spines of rock emerging from the mossy earth, and then finally the four of them were on their butts, scooting down shallow steps carved directly into a sheer cliff. Each step was only a couple feet wide, and the drop on one side went into a foggy nothing.

"This is not where I saw my night going," Mr. Gabler said, as he gingerly navigated where the steps switched back, cutting the opposite way down the cliff face.

"Weird," Agustín said. "This is exactly what I expected."

They all tried to feel okay about what was happening, tried to ignore the dread that had settled on them all. Was Aileen right? Was trying to resist a helpless fight?

"Let's stop dwelling on what we can't do," Esther said.

"Let's talk instead about what we can do."

"If we tried to run, the only place to go would be this Dream of Halloween, which I'd rather not come back to," Mr. Gabler said.

"We can't get to the hospital or anywhere outside of the neighborhood, and everyone inside the neighborhood is asleep," Sasha said.

Esther thought for a second that she saw something green and solid through the mist below them. A sign that they were at least reaching the end of this Dream.

"Hide forever in a bubble of stopped time?" Agustín said.

"Do plants grow when time is stopped?" Sasha said. "Could we even grow food if we needed to?"

"Do we age?" Mr. Gabler said.

"Whoa, so, if we restart time, do we end up dying at an earlier date than otherwise because we spent some time aging in this bubble of stopped time?" Agustín said.

"Either that or you all stay thirteen forever," Mr. Gabler said. "And trust me, you don't want to be thirteen any longer than you have to be."

"Hey!" Sasha said. Then she shrugged. "I mean, you're right."

"Guys, guys, focus," Esther said. She could definitely see land below them. Flashes of green and brown. "I'm not willing to run. Not while our families are trapped in there. Our only option is to fight the queen ourselves."

"Is it our only option if it's not an option?" Agustín said. "She literally has magic powers. We are now talking about someone who is actually preventing the movement of time."

"Esther's right," Sasha said.

Esther looked back at Sasha, but Sasha wasn't meeting her eyes.

"Unexpectedly, I agree," Mr. Gabler said. "We need to fight her. But to do that we need to come up with some sort of plan."

"It's not going to work to just hang around and wait for her to come to us," Esther said. "We need to surprise her where she is."

The bottom of the stairs was clearly visible. There were trees again. She saw orange fruit hanging from them, and worried that they had, through some horrible dream logic, ended up back at the jack-o'-lantern tree. But this was a more familiar orange fruit. It was a grove of orange trees. The moment her foot left the final step, the fog started to clear, and she thought she could feel some transfer in herself, a moment where she actually passed between worlds. Then she was in the orange groves in the hills. It was peaceful up here, the lights of the neighborhood below looked like any normal night. Only the bright orange moon, still in the same place in the sky, told the story of what was actually happening here.

She looked back to see a stone staircase, planted incongruously in between the rows of trees, becoming hazy and transparent as it went up, until it disappeared completely about twenty feet in the air. Gradually, each of her companions appeared—first their feet, then the rest of their bodies, at first see-through and blurry, then sharpening and becoming physical, until they stepped off the last step and became grounded once again in their own world. The moment the last of them touched earth, the steps disappeared completely, leaving behind no sign that they had ever existed.

The four gathered to consider the neighborhood beneath them.

"I think I know where she's staying," Agustín said. He pointed to a patch of darkness among the neat lines of light. Within that darkness was a faint spot of brightness. Not constant and clear like the streetlights and the house lights. Nor distant and twinkling like the stars. Organic and flickering, like a heartbeat.

"That wild party in the canyon," Esther said.

"No high schoolers would have a party that visible," Agustín said. "Or that big. It's not the high schoolers. It's her."

Now with a destination, they hurried down the hillside. All of them, except Mr. Gabler, had snuck into the orange groves regularly growing up, and every kid in the neighborhood knew where the bottom of the fences had been secretly bent back and then replaced, a swinging door not immediately visible to the eyes of the irritated farmers, who invariably chased the kids off the land. Of course, tonight those farmers were in a dream somewhere, and so the groves went unprotected.

They all ducked under the fence, Esther first and then holding it open for the rest.

"I'm not going to ask how you knew where that is," Mr. Gabler said.

"You can totally get us in trouble, but only if you restart time first," Sasha said.

Esther laughed, and Sasha smiled at her in return.

There was no sign of movement, human or otherwise, on their trip to the canyon. The streets were empty. All of the houses were quiet.

They reached the edge of the canyon. From here the light was clearly a fire, or more than one, a huge flickering circle. Voices and movement echoed out from the direction of the flames.

"I'd say that's definitely her," Mr. Gabler said.

"What next?" Sasha said.

"We need to get a closer look," Esther said. "Get an idea of what we're up against."

Sasha considered that for a moment, and then, without saying anything more, started into the canyon. The others hurried to follow.

Esther had had nightmares her whole life of what it would be like, wandering the trails of the canyon in darkness, but now that she was doing it with Agustín and Mr. Gabler and Sasha at her side, it didn't seem that scary. It still seemed very scary. But manageable, rather than the absolute panic that she would feel trying to do it on her own.

She linked arms with Agustín, and all of them started down the slope, until the light from the street faded completely.

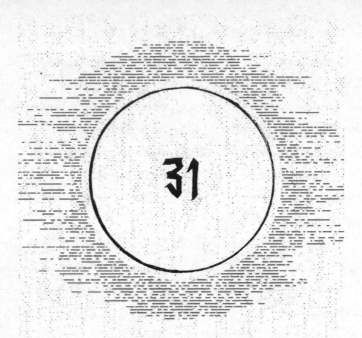

31

EVEN A FEW FEET into the canyon felt like another planet, distant from the comfortable suburbia behind her. During the day, the canyon belonged to Esther. But at night it was a dark canvas that her mind filled with everything that scared her.

She was so grateful for her friends walking beside her. There was no way she would be able to step even one foot down here without them. If they vanished, she would be utterly lost on this winding trail. She held on tighter to Agustín. He didn't seem to mind. He didn't even acknowledge it, which she was a little bit grateful for and a little bit hurt by.

"Let's take this slow," said Mr. Gabler. His limp had faded, but he still winced with every other step. Their feet crunched on the leaves scattered over the trails, making their progress less stealthy than any of them would have liked. The bare trees overhead were skeletons striking strange poses in the moonlight. All of the trails seemed to have a different layout than they had the day before. In the same way that the streets of the town had been changed by this Halloween, the canyon had too.

Sasha inhaled sharply. There were slumped, creeping figures moving on the path ahead.

Esther shushed them all, and drew the group into the brush. They waited, holding their breaths. Three trick-or-treaters—the clown, the dinosaur, and the pirate captain—shambled by. The trick-or-treaters did not talk to each other, only huffed wetly. As their limbs moved, there was a sound like paper rustling.

Once the trick-or-treaters were long past, Esther and the rest made their way carefully out of the brush and back onto the trail.

"I hate those things," said Agustín.

"They didn't choose to become what they are," Esther said. "They're victims just like us."

Agustín shrugged. "You're right. It's hard to remember that when they're buzzing and clicking while trying to kill us, though."

The path continued, winding back on itself. She didn't try to understand where they were. Their destination waited at the heart of this canyon. If they walked long enough, they would reach it.

Then came a new sound. A deep boom that she heard

with her bones more than her ears. They all froze. Another boom, and another, getting louder and louder. This time they hid in the creek bed by the path. The cold stagnant gutter water soaked their clothes, and Esther shivered. The smell of algae filled their nostrils. But none of them complained. None of them moved.

A huge shape took a bite out of the sky. Then another. Every time it moved, entire stretches of stars disappeared from sight. Esther had no idea what she was even looking at. Then the shape moved into the moonlight, and she realized. Now that she knew, she wished that she didn't. She wanted nothing more than for this knowledge to be taken away from her and put somewhere where she would never come across it again.

It was a giant trick-or-treater, several stories tall. This one was dressed as a scarecrow. Every time it moved, its foot landed with that deep boom, sending dust and leaves whirling into the air. The cloud of dust drifted over the creek, and Agustín sneezed. The giant stopped.

To Esther, it felt as though nothing in the entire expanse of the universe dared to move, except her left hand, which trembled.

The giant leaned down. She could see its hideous plastic scarecrow mask, as big as a house. The eyeholes were the size of doors, and she could see nothing but darkness within them. It wavered back and forth, looking for the source of the noise. Esther closed her eyes. If this was the moment she died, she'd rather not see it. Then another boom shook through her bones. She opened her eyes. The giant was walking away.

They crawled out from the creek. It was Mr. Gabler who broke their silence. "Man, I wish I were doing anything but this."

Esther found herself in the confusing position of having to comfort an adult. "None of us want to be doing this. But maybe that's why it's so important that we keep going."

"Yeah," he sighed. "Maybe."

She considered the path they were on. It seemed too dangerous to continue along it when such creatures were guarding the way. But they had to get to the center of the canyon, where the light was. Above the flickering light, she could see a hillside that she recognized. That's when she realized what they were going to have to do, and with that realization she started laughing.

Agustín and Sasha stared in disbelief. Esther could hardly manage to speak she was laughing so hard. The answer had been in front of her the whole time.

"Gus," she wheezed. "Gus. The Feats of Strength."

"What, really?" he said. "Now?" But then he saw what she had seen. The hillside above the source of the flickering light was the ledge above the pond. It was the finish line of their game. And the game completely avoided the monster-filled paths. Esther was right. Their best way through was The Feats of Strength.

"Well," he said. "The tunnel is probably somewhere over this way." It took them a bit to find, since the paths didn't run true, but the tunnel was more or less where it had always been.

"Do we have to climb over?" said Mr. Gabler.

"I don't think we should skip any steps," said Esther, and she started to climb. Sighing, Mr. Gabler followed after. He climbed with a graceful ease, even with his ankle, and she remembered how quickly he had scampered up the side of his house.

Then came the crawl through the drainpipe. This one was particularly hard for Mr. Gabler, who was too big to fit in the narrowest point. But he also had a lot of experience getting through narrow spaces like this, and he expertly wriggled his way out.

"Okay, what next?" Mr. Gabler said. He seemed to be having fun.

"Next we go up there." Agustín pointed. The slope was thick with cacti. Mr. Gabler no longer seemed to be having fun. "Ah, of course," he said.

The way up was as dicey and painful as always, but then came the victory lap, the easy jog along the backside of the fences. Esther noticed that there were no dogs barking from the yards as they ran. Where had all the dogs gone on this ghastly night? This unease was overrun by the joy of finally moving fast, sprinting along the top of this hillside on this path that she and Agustín had made for themselves over years of hanging out together.

Finally the path ended at the ledge. Below the ledge was the silty pond, the final challenge of The Feats of Strength that neither of them had ever dared to actually leap into.

For once, Esther's attention was not on the drop or on the water.

The little clearing around the pond had broadened in the unreal darkness. Now it was a wide meadow. All over it were tents and flagpoles, and everywhere the trick-or-treaters crept, in jack-o'-lantern heads and in tattered Superman jumpsuits and in filthy cowboy outfits. Their faces were never visible. They clicked and squished in unnerving ways. Even worse was what they were doing. There were hundreds of little cots, and on the cots were children kidnapped from the town above. The trick-or-treaters were tending to the sleeping children, with a gentle care that was somehow more terrifying than when they had acted aggressively.

"Yes," said a voice that was rich with authority, and now Esther's eye was drawn to the center of the camp. There a tall and elaborate throne had been constructed, formed of pumpkin vines and bat wings. On it sat the Queen of Halloween, flanked by Dan, crisp paper hat set perfectly on his head, standing stock straight with his arms behind his back, and by Ed, his hat crumpled in his hands, held awkwardly in front of him as he fidgeted and spit.

"The old man almost beefed it for us," said the queen. "That tottering fool. But we were wasting our time with those scattered remnants anyway. Who cares if a few of them are still awake? Right?"

"Absolutely, my queen," soothed Dan. Ed grunted.

"Sure," she said. "Not a problem. No problems. We're all

fine. The children here are all in the Dream. Time is fully stopped. No more will Halloween wax and wane according to the whims of this world's calendar. Now it will be Halloween forever. And I can raise these little children in the Dream, where they will learn what it truly means to be a trick-or-treater."

The trick-or-treaters in the camp cooed and cawed, sharp animal sounds, and Esther had a sickening sense of what they might have once been, before they became these creatures here.

"Sharon is in there somewhere," Esther said. "I know it. We have to rescue her."

"Totally," said Agustín. "This is so creepy. We have to help them."

"I want to rescue my brother as much as any of you. But how, though?" said Sasha, and she had a point. Esther looked out over the camp, full of monsters, not to mention Dan and Ed and their queen, who apparently had the power to stop time and put everyone into an eternal sleep. It wasn't quite the odds Esther would have liked out of the situation.

"A distraction?" she offered.

"Would have to be some distraction," said Sasha. "And even if that happened, how are we going to get all of those kids out of there on our own? And would they even wake up? We don't know how to wake them up yet."

Esther hated that Sasha was right about all of the difficulties. "We can't just give up," Esther said.

"Before we go in there we need to know how to wake them up," said Agustín.

"What's keeping them asleep, exactly?" said Esther.

Sasha pointed at the queen, sitting high on her throne. "I think she is. The Dream of Halloween comes through her. Aileen said that ordinarily the queen shouldn't have this much power. There must be something special she's doing. To wake them up, we need to know what it is."

"Sure, let's ask her," muttered Agustín.

Sasha rolled her eyes. "Look at her hands."

Esther did, and saw what Sasha had already spotted. The queen was cradling a small, shiny black box. Esther remembered that she had been holding that same box in Mr. Nathaniel's driveway. Whatever was in that box was so valuable that the queen wanted to be in contact with it at all times.

"I bet whatever's in that box is necessary for her plan," said Sasha. "Maybe even it's what she gets her new power from."

"I'd love to get it away from her," said Esther. "But that's impossible."

"Not impossible," said Mr. Gabler, who had been sitting out the argument, examining the camp with experienced eyes, checking routes, seeing which areas were more heavily guarded than others. "Very difficult, but not impossible."

"You think you can do it?" said Esther.

He winked. "I wasn't always a dentist, you know."

187

MR. GABLER BIT HIS LIP. The light from the fires of the camp danced across his features, making him look like a different person from one moment to the next.

"This isn't that different from some of the houses that Jimmy Bennington asked me to rob for him back in the day. All of those rich collectors have more security than they know what to do with. Which was good for me, because while they were bumping into each other, I could slip right in and grab what I wanted."

He shook his head. "Sorry. Got a little nostalgic there for a second, but it wasn't a good time in my life." He furrowed his brow and half-heartedly wagged a finger at the kids. "Don't steal."

"Except now," said Esther. "Right now we need you to steal."

"Right. Yeah. I need to steal now. But otherwise." Moral lesson done, he squatted and considered his plan. "So I think I can definitely get in unseen. But obviously she's going to notice when the box is no longer in her hands. And I imagine her reaction might get a little . . . intense."

"She's going to kill us," said Agustín.

"Quite literally, yes," said Mr. Gabler. "Which is why I need you kids to leave."

"What? No," said Sasha. She planted her feet to show how much she wasn't going to move.

"Yeah, we're not going anywhere," said Esther, standing next to Sasha.

"Heck no," said Agustín. "Just, you know, heck no."

"I can't be responsible for putting you kids in this kind of danger," said Mr. Gabler. "I'm not the person I used to be. I'm an actual adult, and I need to do actual adult things. And that means you all need to go right now. I'm not taking any argument."

Esther opened her mouth to offer an argument, but Agustín touched her hand, and his gentle touch made a more persuasive case than any objection she could conjure.

"Okay, Mr. Gabler," he said. "You're right. We'll go."

"We will?" said Esther.

"No we won't," said Sasha.

"Yes, we're going." Agustín made slow eye contact with both of them, and Esther got it. She looked back at Mr. Gabler with amazement. She had so completely misjudged him as boring and sad. She wondered how much of what she knew about the world was wrong. That thought felt like drowning, but also in some small way it felt wonderful. There was so much still to learn.

"Let's go, Sasha," she said.

Sasha stayed where she was while the others retreated up the hill. Her chin trembled a little as she tried to hold in her tears. "I'm sorry, Mr. Gabler. I thought we all were brave."

"Oh, Sasha, you are brave." Sasha sobbed a little and hugged Mr. Gabler. He patted her back and said, "You are braver than I've been at any age. Now follow the others." Sasha nodded and jogged after Esther and Agustín, who were waiting for her up the hill.

"Do you trust us?" Esther asked Sasha when she reached them.

Sasha formed her mouth to say no and then realized that wasn't true anymore. She nodded. Esther grabbed her hand. She thought about all the hurt that had passed between them. Cruelty and mistruths and anger. She squeezed Sasha's hand. The two of them were caught in something heavy and tangled and vast, and the only way out was for them to escape it together.

"Okay, here's the plan," Esther said.

Mr. Gabler turned back to the camp. He pulled from his pocket the small, sharp stone that had started this night by waking him up. The stone had brought back memories he hadn't wanted to think about in years, but it was also a reminder: He could do this. He had done this before. But he would need one major distraction.

It turned out he wasn't the only one who had realized this, because Esther and Agustín and Sasha came running into the clearing. All three of them shouted and waved their arms.

"Hey, weirdos! Over here!"

"You can't catch us!"

Everyone in camp turned to see what the ruckus was about. Dan rolled his eyes. The trick-or-treaters clicked and buzzed, seeming unsure of what to do. The queen went red with fury.

"Get them! Bring them to me!" she howled.

Most of the trick-or-treaters dutifully squirmed their way across the camp toward the three kids, who disappeared back into the brush. Dan and Ed glanced at the queen, and, seeing her mood, also ran in that direction.

Mr. Gabler was annoyed and worried, and at first he started down to help the three of them escape their pursuers. But he realized that then they would all be right back where they had started. No, as bad an idea as it had been for them to try to help him, they had given him an opportunity, and it would be wrong not to take it. He closed his eyes, slowing his breath and his heart rate, the same way he would before any big job back in his days of stealing from museums and wealthy collectors. Then he opened his eyes and slipped gracefully down the hillside.

He kept to the shadows, moving when the fire guttered in the wind, so if anyone saw him, he would appear to be an aspect of light. The few trick-or-treaters left in camp were staring off in the direction that all the others had run. The queen, too, was standing atop her throne, trying to see what was going on. Halfway through camp he started to get confident and moved into a run. Which was when he almost smacked right into the back of a trick-or-treater dressed as a robot. The spray-painted cardboard boxes that made up its body were soggy and seamed with black lines of rot. Up close, Mr. Gabler caught a whiff of a pungent odor like a sponge left wet for too long. Cleaning fluid and mold. The thing started to turn, and Mr. Gabler fell backward, landing softly on his hands and rolling under one of the cots holding a child. The trick-or-treater shuffled over and made a series of wet popping sounds. Mr. Gabler held his breath.

"Faster!" Esther shouted from far away. The robot-costumed creature turned at the sound and shuffled away. Mr. Gabler hoped that the kids were still safe. He rolled back to his feet and started again for the throne. This time he was careful, but he also knew his window was closing. He didn't have much time left.

He reached the throne, crouching behind it.

"Bring them now! Bring them now!" the queen shrieked from just above him. How was he going to get the box out of her hands? This was a nearly impossible problem that he had less than a minute to solve. He looked frantically around him.

On either side of the throne were piles of fruit, Dan's

red apples on one side and Ed's enormous orange pumpkins on the other. Mr. Gabler reached out and grabbed one of the pumpkins. He wondered if it would work for him, or if it was somehow tied to Ed, but no, the pumpkin caught afire, flames as cartoonishly orange as the fruit they sprouted from. Mr. Gabler squeaked in pain and surprise, and without thinking through the repercussions, he tossed the projectile directly onto the queen's throne.

The throne, made of dry organic material, went up in seconds. A roaring pillar of flame. The queen leapt off, but parts of her dress carried the fire with her, and she swatted at them, yelping. This was Mr. Gabler's only chance. He darted through the smoke, shoved her over, and yanked the box out of her hand as she fell.

"How dare you!" the queen squalled, but Mr. Gabler was already sprinting. There was no time for stealth now. His ankle felt like a sharp jangle of broken glass, but he ignored it, put his head down, and dashed into the night.

"Back to me! Back to your queen! Get the thief. He has stolen the moon! He has stolen the moon!"

Her voice no longer sounded quite like a person's. Her rage was distorting it, and there was something larger and older than humankind in her voice. If the night could talk, it would sound like that. If Halloween could talk, it would sound like that.

"Esther! Agustín! Sasha!" Mr. Gabler shouted as he flew. Miraculously, the three of them popped out of the brush thirty feet down the path. He looked back and saw that the trick-or-treaters were all swarming after him. Most terrifyingly of all, he felt the subsonic boom of the giant scarecrow. Its towering silhouette loomed out of the night from the trees next to him.

"Quick!" said Mr. Gabler. "Catch!" And he launched the box, hoping it would be visible enough for them to retrieve. Esther reached out her hands and, with no athletic ability and never having played an organized sport, managed to catch it in her wild arms. She started forward to join Mr. Gabler, but he shook his head frantically. "No! Get out of here!"

Just then, as if to emphasize the point, the giant's hand flung itself out of the woods and scooped him up. Mr. Gabler was held, squirming, up to the hollow sack eyes of the scarecrow's massive face. A little sharp stone fell from his pocket to the dark path below, the last bit of luck leaving him. As it fell, it glowed a bright and vivid orange, a tiny shooting star until it fizzled out in the dirt of the path.

"No," Sasha whispered.

They could hear the deep drone of the queen's new voice though the trees and the brush and the hills.

"Into the Dream. I banish him into the Dream."

As quick and indisputable as a door slamming shut, consciousness left Mr. Gabler, and he was as gone as every other adult in town. Deep in the restless sleep of the Dream.

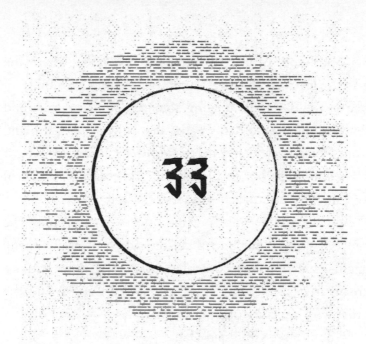

33

"MR. GABLER!" CRIED ESTHER, but Sasha and
Agustín were already pulling her down the trail.

"Come on, Est, we've got to go," said Agustín. "Mr.
Gabler wouldn't have wanted us to get caught."

"Because then who would be around to rescue him?"
said Sasha.

They were right. Esther, burying the shame it gave her,
turned away from the camp and ran. The pack of hungry
trick-or-treaters took after them, horrible clicking and snuf-
fling sounds coming from beneath their masks and robes.
The giant, at least, had turned and was lumbering back to
camp with the sleeping body of Mr. Gabler.

"To the street!" Esther said, not sure that the street
would be any safer. But she wanted out of the dark path-
ways of this canyon, back to the familiar lights of her

neighborhood. At least there she would know where she was. At least on the street there wasn't the possibility of one of the dirt trails turning some unfamiliar corner and drawing them onto darks paths that only existed at night, from which they would never find their way home. No, it was better to be out on the asphalt and concrete of a small and simple place that she understood well.

So they sprinted up the steep slope to the gate of the canyon, spilling out into a cul-de-sac. Waiting for them, engines purring like contented predators, were two ice cream trucks, one with the picture of an apple, and the other with a picture of a pumpkin.

"Good to see you," said Dan.

"Yeah, good to see you," said Ed.

Dan shot a glare at his brother. "I already said that."

"Well, I can say it too. We can both say it."

"Find your own thing to say."

"I did. It happened to be the same as yours."

"Unbelievable."

Maybe they would have bickered all night, letting the kids sneak past, but a howl of fury came from the darkness of the canyon. This caused the brothers to snap their attention back to the situation at hand. Esther grasped tightly to the mysterious box that Mr. Gabler had sacrificed his freedom to retrieve. Whatever was inside it was the key to this never-ending Halloween, and she wasn't about to let down her friends by losing it.

As if reading her mind, Ed's eyes rested on what she was holding, and he frowned.

"Not yours," he grunted. "Stealing."

"Very naughty," agreed Dan. He produced a shiny red apple from his pocket, and with a friendly wink at the children, caused shiny razor blades to grow from it. Ed took up a pumpkin by its stem, and it bloomed into flame.

"Time to give it back," said Dan, and Esther tensed herself for the onslaught. She wasn't sure what she would do, only that she wasn't going to go down without trying something. Her mind raced for ideas, but she found every avenue of her brain disconcertingly blank. She didn't seem to know what to do at all.

And then: "Yergeherrer!" someone called, a nonsense phrase of adrenaline and aggression, and someone's body launched itself at the brothers, a lanky cannonball. It was Sasha.

"Sasha, wait!" shouted Agustín, but there was no waiting for Sasha. She had years of anger at the way the world had treated her, and for once she wasn't taking out that anger on an innocent bystander.

"What is the child doing?" whispered Ed.

"I don't know," Dan whispered. There was a sour note of panic in his voice, and he tried to cover it with his usual smoothness, but it wouldn't quite go. "No child has ever done this before."

Which was when Sasha reached him and, with the years of experience being the most aggressive soccer player on her team, swept his legs out from under him.

"Agh!" cried Dan. To his complete shock, he found himself on his back, with this little girl on his chest, kicking and punching. Where had his apple gone? He couldn't seem to find it. Well, never mind, there was an infinite amount in his truck and in his pockets. But—and this was some concern—he couldn't seem to reach either of those. So he didn't have any way of stopping his attacker from continuing to hurt him quite badly.

Ed had been struck utterly still with surprise, but he recovered himself. He couldn't throw the flaming pumpkin, not with his brother right there, so he tossed it aside and went to grab Sasha. At that point, unfortunately for Ed, Agustín had gotten the idea, and he rammed his shoulder into Ed's side.

"Whoa, I had no idea I could do that," said Agustín. He had laid Ed out flat without thinking through what he was going to do at all.

Sasha was now jumping up and down on Dan, and Dan didn't like that one bit. He tried once more for his apples, and retrieved one, but before the blades could sprout, Esther ran up and kicked it out of his hand.

"Come on!" shouted Dan in frustration.

"Come on!" shouted Agustín to his friends, as he pushed Ed back down before the big man could get up and grab any of his flaming squash.

The three of them ran away past the trucks, as the two brothers slowly pulled themselves up, cursing, wondering what had just happened to them.

Esther gestured the other two into the side yard of a house where they hid to study the box. "I think we've lost them for a moment. We need to get this open."

The latch was a complex series of cubes that seemed on the verge of opening but would not budge. Esther felt a mix of panic and frustration fizzing through her as she started fumbling with the cubes.

"Hold on," said Agustín. "I used to have a puzzle like that. I think I know the trick."

He took the box up, studied the latch carefully, nodded to himself, then yanked at the lid as hard as he could, and the box snapped open with a loud crack.

He shrugged. "I was never great at puzzles."

The interior was a rich red velvet. At the center was a moon rock, stolen from the Bennington Museum of the Unusual and Rare (before which it had been stolen by a petty thief named Gene Gabler from a van in a UCLA parking lot). A little label in the box identified it as *Sea of Tranquility. 1971.*

"Whoa," said Esther. She pulled the rock out of the box and held it up.

As if responding to her touch, or maybe to her voice, or maybe to the light of the moon, the moon rock glowed a dazzling orange. Esther felt herself drawn to the rock in her hand. She felt dizzy.

"Oh no," she said.

"What's happening?" said Sasha.

"Yeah, what's—" started Agustín, but he never got to finish.

All three of them fell fast asleep, and right away began to dream.

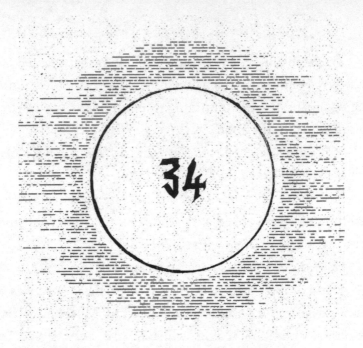

34

ESTHER GOLD LOVED HALLOWEEN.

She loved looking in the mirror and seeing a monster
looking back at her. She loved the weight of a heavy bag of
candy in her hands. She loved jack-o'-lanterns and plastic
gravestones with bad puns on them. She loved movies in
which people made poorly thought-out decisions and then
were immediately punished for those decisions by a super-
natural creature or a masked maniac wielding a machete.

And today she was happy, because today was Halloween.

"Have fun trick-or-treating," her dad said. He was at
the piano. She loved when he played piano. Instrumental
improvisation on some pop song from the seventies, or
sometimes just scales for hours at a time. Her earliest memories were lying in bed, faintly hearing her father playing
scales late into the night. She was so glad that he was back

at an instrument she liked hearing.

"Yes, honey, we can't wait to see what costumes you make when you go out next year," her mom said. Her mom, usually stressed out about work, seemed so relaxed, like Esther rarely saw except when the family went on vacation. Her face was loose, her smile easy.

"You don't mind me still trick-or-treating next year?" Esther said.

"Oh no, of course not," her dad said, playing a series of rising major chords on the piano.

"And the year after that, and the year after that," her mom sang in tune with the piano. In fact, Esther realized, everything that her father and mother had said so far had been sung. Esther thought that there was something wrong here. She struggled to figure out what it was.

But she couldn't hold on to the thought. The moment she had it, it was already gone.

"Say, want to hear me play saxophone?" her dad sang, pulling the saxophone out of the open top of the grand piano.

"Oh, Dad, that's okay," she said, edging toward the door, but he already had it to his mouth. And he played, and it was beautiful—perfectly modulated notes, on pitch, a clear tone. She could have listened to him for hours. He played a short song, a catchy, upbeat tune that she didn't recognize.

"See. I finally got it. No more torturing you all with my practicing. I have it perfectly now."

"I love it," her mom trilled, without a trace of sarcasm.

She leaned back in the dining room chair and sighed. "Isn't life great?"

"Plus I wrote that song," her dad said.

"He wrote it," her mom said. "Isn't that lovely?"

"That's really cool!" Esther said. Her dad always liked writing music, but he had trouble finding the time or inspiration. He would sometimes be down on himself, a musician who only made a living playing tired dance songs from decades ago for partygoers who didn't know good music from bad. He had always wanted to be a songwriter, an artist with a capital A.

"I wrote that!" he said again. He seemed years younger. Like, literally years younger. Esther realized that both he and her mom were in their early thirties at most. That wasn't right. That wasn't the age they were. But again, she couldn't hold on to that thought. *What was I just thinking?* she wondered, but brushed it off. If it was important, she would remember.

"Alright, I'm going!" she said.

She felt a weight in her hand and realized that she was holding a weird gray rock. She studied it. It was familiar, but she couldn't place where she had seen it. *Oh well,* she thought, *I'll figure it out after tonight,* and slipped it in her pocket.

As she went to the front door, she looked in the hall mirror and gasped in awe. This was her best costume yet, by far.

In the mirror, she was ten feet tall, in a dark reaper's

cloak. Her face, such as was visible under the cloak's hood, was covered in thin, pale skin, almost transparent, her teeth protruding and sharp, her muscles and veins visible. She was a horrifying apparition, from the depth of her worst nightmares. When she looked down at herself, she was just her, at her own height, with her own body, but in the mirror she loomed. In the mirror, she was a creature from the best kind of movie. It was everything she had ever wanted from a costume.

She opened the door and practically skipped outside. She couldn't remember a time she was ever this excited to get started. But she stopped, confused. This wasn't her neighborhood. She was at the top of a tall cliff, all dark rock, no vegetation, a barren, lifeless landscape. There was a single dead tree next to her, as black as the rock, burned or petrified into a skeleton, its branches zigzagging against a sky that seemed to have no stars at all, only a faint, even gray glow. And, looming over all the rest, a giant orange moon, bigger than she thought was possible. It took over the entirety of one hemisphere of the sky, an angry orange, so close she could see its craters and valleys. Below, at the bottom of the impossibly tall cliff was a deep and churning ocean. Its water swallowed light, an impenetrable darkness, with only the rumble of waves crashing into rock, vicious and dangerous, to let her know what was down there. The only visual clue was the reflection of the moon, which scattered out over the surface, turning the massive waves orange and then not. Orange and then not. Like a light turning on and off. She couldn't breathe. Where was she? She whirled around, desperate for any way down from this lonely perch and—

She was standing at the bottom of the front steps of her house. Cradled in her hands was an orange bag with a jack-o'-lantern pattern.

"Well go on," her dad called to her from the front door. "Go out and get that candy."

Esther tried to clear her head. There had been something else, after leaving her house. She had just seen something wrong, but she couldn't remember what it was. She decided to forget it and headed to the first house down the street.

"Well, isn't that a nifty costume," the old woman wearing a witch hat said to her, and poured out her entire bowl of candy into Esther's bag.

"Whoa," Esther said.

The woman winked. "Little bonus for having the best costume of the night," she said as she closed the door.

Every door she went to, people were so impressed with her costume. She was getting more candy than she had ever gotten, but her bag never got any heavier. It felt basically empty, but when she opened it, it contained a bottomless pit of foil-covered chocolates and neon candy wrappers.

Mr. Gabler was out on his front porch. He waved to her, and she waved back.

"Oh, hi there, Esther," he said.

"Hello, Mr. Gabler."

"Having a good Halloween?"

"Yes, Mr. Gabler."

"Well, I've got something that'll make it even better."

She sighed as he picked up the red plastic bowl he kept his usual Halloween toothpaste in. But this time he pulled out a giant chocolate bar, so big that she wasn't sure how it had fit in the bowl.

"Oh wow," she said, taking the bar from him. It was as heavy as a backpack full of textbooks, but as soon as she dropped it into her bag, the weight disappeared. "That's a little different from your usual."

"I don't think it matters here," Mr. Gabler said.

"What do you mean by that?"

Mr. Gabler laughed. "I don't know. I have no idea. I don't think it matters here. Come back anytime you want another."

He leaned back and looked up at the sky. His face became suddenly terrified. There was orange light on his skin. She followed his gaze. Nearly the entire sky was taken up by a huge, orange moon. She heard violent, crashing waves.

Then she was on to the next set of houses. The people in her neighborhood had really gone all out on their decorations. There were complex pumpkin carvings, the usual crude faces replaced with photorealistic portraits and entire horror movie scenes carefully carved and then brought to life with the flicker of a candle. Even houses that usually merely left a porch light on now had fake graveyards, full of fake skeletons and propped-up mummies. She wondered how Mr. Winchell, the neighborhood King of Halloween

Decorations, felt about the new competition.

But she didn't have to wonder for long, because the next house was Mr. Winchell's, and he had earned his title once again. His yard seemed to be ten times as big as it used to be, acres of dense Halloween decorations sprawling out in every direction. There were entire fake villages, full of heavy-browed, scowling townsfolk, watched over by crumbling ancient castles whose lords lived eternal, unnatural lives. There was a dark forest, in which glowing eyes blinked on and off in the fog, and from which echoed the howl of fearsome beasts. And what had once been a few pieces of plywood set up in a crude tunnel was now an entire hedge maze leading to his front door.

She made her way through the hedge maze, deliciously spooked by the whispers and movement she could hear on the other side of the hedges, of the shrouded figures she could see disappearing around corners right ahead of her. All of this set to the music of her favorite horror movies, not played over a recording, but live, an entire orchestra somewhere in the massive yard.

Finally she made it to the door and knocked. "Trick or treat," she said as the door swung open with a lovely, ominous creak.

"Esther!" Mr. Winchell said. As usual, he was not dressed up. He liked to dress his house in costume, not himself. He poked his glasses back in place and waved proudly around him. "I was hoping you'd come by. What do you think?"

"It's amazing, Mr. Winchell. I've never seen anything like it."

"I've outdone myself this year. This is the best it's ever been. I had so many new ideas, and they all flowed so easily."

"How did you even manage to put it all up on your own?" she said.

He frowned. "You know, Esther, I don't remember." He shook his head. "I just don't remember."

They stood in silence for a moment. There was something that both of them could almost recall, but neither of them could quite put their finger on what it was.

"Well, it's incredible," she said finally, letting go of whatever that distracting thought had been. The tension in Mr. Winchell's face broke.

"Yes, I'm very proud. Thanks for coming by. Oh, and I almost forgot."

He reached over and hauled up a huge sack of candy.

"Incoming!" he said, and poured out the entire sack into her bag. The candy flowed, and flowed, and flowed, but her bag didn't get any heavier.

"There," he said, once the sack was empty. "That ought to do it. See you next Halloween, Esther."

"See you, Mr. Winchell."

Somehow she made it back to the street without having to pass through the lengthy maze again. She couldn't understand exactly how she had done that, but it didn't seem important.

She looked into her bag. She had never seen that much candy in one place. It was probably time to call it a night. How fun trick-or-treating was. She would never give it up.

As she headed home, she saw a girl standing on the

sidewalk, gazing forlornly down the street.

"Sasha?" Esther said.

Sasha turned. Her face was wet, and her eyes were puffy. It looked like she had been crying for hours.

"Have you seen my mom? She was supposed to pick me up here, but she hasn't come by."

Esther looked up and down the street and realized that she hadn't seen a single car the entire time she had been out.

"No. But I'm sure she'll come soon. Do you want to wait at my house?"

"That's okay," Sasha said. "I'm supposed to wait here, I think. I think I'm just supposed to keep waiting. I think I've been waiting a long time."

"Are you alright?" Esther touched her arm with concern. Sasha nodded, but the tears kept flowing.

"I'm fine, I think. Or I don't know what to think. Is this right? Is this how it's supposed to be?"

"Sure," Esther said. "What could be wrong about it? Look how much fun everyone's having."

She gestured at the houses with their brightly lit decorations, and the groups of trick-or-treaters moving between them, laughing, with buckets full of candy. But instead she found herself gesturing at a dark and churning ocean. She was on a tall cliff made of black rock, next to a dead tree. The moon took up most of the sky. It didn't seem possible that the moon could ever be that big. She looked over the edge of the cliff and felt dizzy. Nothing terrified her more than that ocean below, and whatever lurked within it. This was not an ocean on Earth, she knew. Whatever unimaginable creatures lived in there had never been seen by human eyes. She could feel the hunger, not from the creatures, but from the water itself. It wanted her to fall, it wanted her to splash, it wanted her to drown.

"Where is this?" she screamed, turning back to Sasha. Sasha wasn't there. Esther was on her street again, alone. Her house was right there, on the corner. A laughing pack of trick-or-treaters ran past her.

"This is the best Halloween night ever!" one of them shouted.

And it was, wasn't it? She felt happy again. She didn't know why she would have ever felt otherwise.

Contentedly, she went up her front steps and through her front door. Her dad was at the piano, and her mom was in the living room.

"Hi, sweetheart," her mom said. "How did it go out there?"

"It was so fun!"

"That's great, just great," her dad said. "Hey, want to hear something?"

He started playing a song. It was the same song he had been playing on the saxophone, but it had been expanded upon. He added counterpoint with the left hand, and another section that balanced out the rapid melody of the first part with slow, simple harmonies.

"I wrote that," he said. "That's a song I wrote. It finally came to me."

"It was so good, Dad," she said. It really was.

"I love it when he plays that song," her mom said. She looked even more relaxed than before. The recliner was all the way back, and her mom's expression was a haze of happiness.

"Hey, don't you want to get out there?" her dad said.

"Get out where?" she said.

"Trick-or-treating, of course," her mom said.

"But I was just . . ." She looked down into the bag. It was empty. And she remembered that it was Halloween, and she was about to go trick-or-treating. She got so excited. This was her favorite time of the year.

She felt a weight in her hand and realized that she was holding a weird gray rock. *I know this rock. It's really important to remember what this rock is.* But she couldn't, and so she dismissed the thought and slipped the rock into her pocket.

As she went to the front door, she looked in the hall mirror, and gasped in awe. This was her best costume yet, by far.

In the mirror, she was an entire crowd of ghostly children. There were more than one of her, with different horrifying faces, transparent bodies, dressed in old-fashioned school uniforms. She didn't know how she managed to make herself look like more than one person, but it was extraordinary. She had outdone herself.

Waiting outside was an older woman. It took a second for Esther to recognize her, because she was livelier than Esther had seen in years. "Grandma Debbie!" she called.

"Oh, Esther," Debbie said, taking her hand. Grandma's

skin was dry and warm. "Isn't tonight wonderful? Isn't it the best night of the year?"

"It absolutely is." It seemed wrong to Esther that Debbie was here. "Grandma, you haven't taken me trick-or-treating in years."

"I know, I know," said Debbie. She smelled like candy corn and smoke. "We need to make up for lost time. Come on!" She pulled at Esther's hand.

Everyone who answered their door was impressed with her costume and told her so. Debbie waited at the sidewalk, beaming, and then together they would look at what candy Esther got and debate its merits. They walked by Mr. Gabler's house. He wasn't out, but his chair and his red bowl were. The red bowl was full of water. The water smelled like seawater. Esther put her hand in and swished it around, but there was nothing, so they continued on, her hand dripping as she walked.

Then they were on to the next set of houses. The people in her neighborhood had really gone all out on their decorations. There were fully acted out scenes, performed by hundreds of actors, in nearly every yard. Even houses that usually merely left a porch light on now had been rebuilt into tall and teetering Victorian mansions, with ghostly pale faces staring bleakly from the windows. Grandma Debbie oohed and aahed with gusto, pointing at each house as it came and saying "Esther, look!" as though Esther hadn't seen. She wondered how Mr. Winchell, the neighborhood King of Halloween Decorations, felt about the new competition.

But Mr. Winchell's yard did not disappoint. His yard

stretched for what looked like hundreds of miles. On one end was a full-sized mountain range in which tall, hairy creatures with hard black eyes roamed, tossing ice boulders down on screaming climbers. By the house there was an aquarium in which a shark swam, and a squid the size of a passenger plane, with a single eye staring out with furious hatred at the world. It was the biggest and most frightening animal Esther had ever seen.

The usual plywood maze had been replaced by a train, a steam locomotive hauling old-fashioned passenger cars.

"Go on," Grandma Debbie said. "I'll be waiting right here."

The train carried Esther for hours across mile after mile of scenes and scenarios Mr. Winchell had created for Halloween. The train was a ghost train, full of ghost passengers who stared out at the landscape with hollow shadows where eyes usually are.

"This is the best it's ever been," she told Mr. Winchell when he answered the door.

He looked harried. "Yeah, I don't even know how I came up with it. It's so big. How did I build it, you know?" He laughed, but the laugh sounded panicked. "How did I even build it?"

She didn't know what to say to that.

"Well, here you go," he said, and pulled out a bag of chocolate nearly as big as he was. He tossed it to her with a grunt, and despite its size she caught it easily. "Bye now." He shut the door.

"Bye, Mr. Winchell. Thank you." She turned and walked the few short steps back to the street. The way back seemed much shorter than the trip there had been, but maybe she had misremembered. She took Grandma Debbie's hand and continued down the street. As she did, she noticed unusual structures behind the houses. Long, rounded bases, and then four gigantic towers that went up and up. Her eyes followed the full length of one tower, and she realized it was a leg. The four towers were the legs of Mr. Gabler and Sasha Min, standing on opposite sides of the street, facing each other. They were thousands of feet tall.

"Huh," Esther said. That didn't seem right, but her brain couldn't hold on to it, and her grandma was already pulling her forward enthusiastically.

She continued to Spindrift Court and found the house that always had the haunted house in the backyard. This house had also improved considerably. The haunted house was now bigger than the home it was attached to. There was an entire staff of costumed employees, ushering thrill seekers inside. A clown with a chainsaw ran around the line, scaring people into embarrassed giggles. She had always dreamed of visiting a haunted house like this, and now there was one just a couple blocks from her home.

"Hey," Agustín called out. He was standing in the door of the main house, where the parents were having their grown-up Halloween party. Esther looked at Grandma Debbie, a little shy, but Debbie just patted her cheek.

"Go on," she whispered. "I'll be waiting right here."

Esther turned away from her grandma and joined Agustín in the entryway.

"What are you doing in here?" she said.

"I don't know." He looked around at the rooms of chatting adults holding wineglasses, as though it were a mystery he could solve. "I remembered there being something wrong about this party, and I wanted to see. But everything seems fine."

"More than fine," she said. "Isn't this the best Halloween ever? And it's even better now that I'm spending it with you."

This was more direct than they had ever been with each other, especially in the last couple years, but she was so genuinely happy to see him that she forgot to hide how she felt. She hugged him, which she had never done. He didn't seem to know what to do, but then he hugged her back.

"It's pretty good, yeah," he said. "But there's something. I don't know." He looked again at the party, as though hoping it would be different if he caught it by surprise. "Let's go upstairs, see if there's anything there."

She followed him up the stairs. On the landing was a window. Through the window, she could see a huge orange moon. It seemed to be right on the other side of the glass. And below it was a dark ocean, so deep as to be basically bottomless. If she ever touched that ocean, even with just one toe, she would be lost forever. She would be dragged down, and down, and down.

She turned away from the window and forgot what she had been looking at, although her arms still prickled as though she were touching something frozen. "Do you like Halloween any better?" she asked.

Agustín looked back at her, his face utterly earnest. His

sincerity made her heart crack a little, but in a way she found strangely nice.

"No. But it's okay, I don't have to. I like that you like it."

She knew that he was right. He didn't have to like Halloween because she did. This shouldn't have felt like a revelation, and yet it struck her as one.

And then they were past the landing, onto the second floor. It seemed completely normal. A few bedrooms. One of which had been converted into an office.

"I don't know, everything looks fine to me," she said.

"I know what it looks like. But there's more to it than what it looks like."

He was so serious and concerned, and she felt something slip in her chest. It felt physical, an actual movement, some part of her shifting and making room for a new version of herself.

"I want to kiss you now," she said.

"Okay," he said.

She took him by the shoulders and kissed him. Then she pulled back to see how he would react. His eyes were wide, but then they relaxed and he kissed her back.

"I like you," she said. "I mean, obviously, you're my friend, but I *like* you, like you."

"I like you too," he said. "I think maybe I have for a while."

"Yeah. Definitely for a while. Me too."

"Why didn't we ever talk like this before? Why didn't we say that to each other?"

"I think we didn't know what it was," she said. "I think

215

we were friends for so long before these feelings came, and we didn't know what they were."

"And why do we know now?" he said.

"I don't know," she said. "It's different now. It feels like . . . like . . ."

"Like a dream," he said.

"Yeah, like a dream," she said, and leaned in to kiss him again. Now that she had done it once, she wanted to do it over and over. She maybe liked kissing more than she liked trick-or-treating, more than scary movies, more than Halloween itself, a realization that would have horrified her just a few minutes before. But when she leaned in, he was gone. She was alone.

"Hello?" she said.

"Hi there," her mother said.

Esther was back in her own house. Had she been some-where else? She didn't think so. Now she remembered. She was home and about to go out for her favorite holiday.

"Happy Halloween," her mom said. She was on the couch with the TV on. Esther didn't recognize the show. It seemed to just be a continuous shot of a huge orange moon, broken by occasional bursts of static. The static sounded like ocean waves. A cold mist drifted out of the TV. Esther tasted salt in the air.

"Are you ready to go trick-or-treating?" her dad said. He had constructed a makeshift recording studio in the liv-ing room. "I'm going to record my song while you're out. Maybe you can listen after."

Esther felt a weight in her hand and realized that she was holding a weird gray rock. *Don't put it away,* she thought. *You have to remember what it is.*

"But I was out. I went trick-or-treating. Grandma was there, I think. I was just . . ." Whatever she had been saying was gone. She couldn't hold on to it. Except one thing. She remembered Agustín. When she remembered him, there was a pang inside her, as if she were a string that had just been plucked. That pang kept the memory from slipping away. She remembered climbing stairs with him. She didn't remember where they were. She remembered them talking, but not what they had talked about. And then she remembered a kiss. She could feel his lips, and the memory clicked back in place, as solid as it had been before. The memory of kissing Agustín couldn't be taken from her. It had been perfect. It had been like—

"Like a dream," she said. The rock grew heavier in her palm.

"What was that?" her mom said.

"Nothing, Mom. I think I'm going to stay in tonight." She caught a look at herself in the mirror. The costume was even better than before. She was an incomprehensible seething cloud of shape and light, dazzling to the eye. She didn't even look human. It was amazing. "Yeah, trick-or-treating is fun, but I think maybe I'm too old for that."

She heard waves crashing onto rocks.

"You? Too old?" Her dad wrinkled his brow. "Never thought I'd hear you say that. Are you feeling okay?"

"Do you have a fever, dear?" her mom said.

"No, I'm fine. I'm more than fine." She sat down next to her mom on the couch. The moon on the TV was closer and brighter than before. It seemed to go beyond the edges of the screen. The sound of waves was loud, so loud it was difficult to hear herself talk. "I think what I need in this situation is something new. I think I need to do things differently, break the rut I've been stuck in. I think it's time for me to change."

The rock grew warm in her hand.

"But you love trick-or-treating," her dad said.

"Yes, no one loves Halloween more than you," her mom said.

"That's true," she said. "But I think I'm done with it. I think I'm ready for whatever happens next."

The rock in her hand now was so hot it was painful. The windows of the house broke. Black seawater poured in from all directions. In three terrifying seconds, she was completely submerged.

Esther Gold woke up.

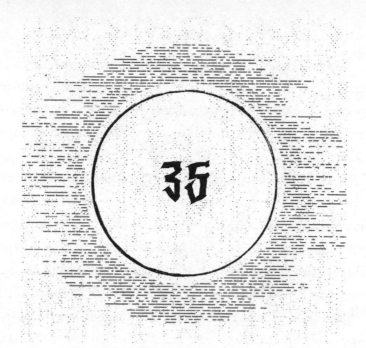

ESTHER WAS LYING IN the grass between Agustín and Sasha, holding the moon rock to her chest.

"Hey," she said, sitting up. She shook Agustín, and then Sasha. "Hey." But they didn't wake up. There wasn't even a flicker to their eyelids. They were still in the Dream.

She got up. Her legs were stiff and cramped under her. She had been out for a while. She didn't know how long. Hours at least. Maybe even days. She was so thirsty. The moon was still on the horizon, in the exact same place it had been before.

Taking stock of her situation, it didn't seem great, if she was honest. All of her friends were still asleep, as were her parents and every other adult in town. Her siblings were missing. Time wasn't moving. And the moon rock they had taken hadn't been enough to protect them from the power of the queen.

On the other hand, she had managed to wake herself up. And if she could wake herself up, then the queen's power over them wasn't absolute. There were weaknesses and loopholes. She had to find them. She just had no idea where to start.

Well, start somewhere. Start with doing anything, and then try to figure out what to do next. So she walked back toward the canyon, leaving the others to slumber under the unchanging moon. The trail led down into the shadows of the canyon, and she was horribly aware of how alone she was. The canyon had been scary in the dark, but now with no one else, it was impossible. She turned, searching for any other option.

And, as if by a miracle, there was light and movement nearby, in a little clearing mostly hidden by trees. She made her way toward it cautiously, in case it was the queen or any of her minions. But it was not the queen. She peered through branches to see her brother surrounded by cheering fellow high schoolers. She pushed through the branches, came out in the clearing. There was a bonfire and empty cans everywhere. Esther studied the cans, her heart beating suddenly cold. Each was pink and had a flattering portrait of the Queen of Halloween. *Pure Dream*, the label said, and underneath that *Live Like a Dream . . . Forever!*

There were teenagers, so many of them, chatting and laughing in tight groups on the edges of the party, but Esther only cared about one of them.

"Ben," she shouted. His eyes went wide.

"Esther? What are you doing here? You shouldn't be here."

The other teenagers stared at her, faces hovering between confusion and animosity. She knew she was the kid at the party, an unwelcome intrusion.

"Ben, please, you have to help me."

"Okay," he said. He put his arm around her shoulder. "Okay, sure. What's going on, Esther? What's wrong?"

What was wrong? Where to start? How to even summarize everything that had happened?

Start with what's important.

"Sharon," she said. "Sharon is missing."

"Sharon?" There was something slow in his reaction, clumsy in his facial expressions.

"Right. Sharon has been taken by someone. Mom and Dad can't help. They're . . . they can't help. We need to get Sharon back. I need your help, Ben."

He nodded earnestly.

"Wait here," he said. "I know what to do."

He got up and strode with purpose across the clearing. She felt something loosen in her rib cage. Now it wasn't all on her. She wasn't the one in charge anymore. The piece of the moon felt heavy in her hands, but her older brother would take care of her.

Ben tapped the shoulders of one of the boys. He talked urgently to him. The others in the group got involved. One of the girls nodded, reached into a cooler, and handed Ben one of the pink cans. He jogged back across the clearing.

"Here," he said. "Drink this." The portrait of the queen on the can seemed to sneer at her. *Pure Dream*, it promised. *Forever*, it promised.

"What?" Esther said. "No. Sharon's missing."

"Come on," he said. "Have some fun. It's a party."

"Yeah, loosen up," called the girl who had given Ben the can.

"Did you hear what I said? Our little sister is missing."

"Sharon's missing?" Ben looked concerned again, but his expression was slow. All of the teenagers had something vacant about their faces.

Ben got up, looked around as though searching for what to do next, and then offered her the can again.

"Not used to seeing you at a party," he said. "But maybe you're getting old enough. Let me introduce you around."

She began to cry. Everyone in this clearing was caught in a different kind of dream, a waking dream. All of the teenagers were in a party that had been going on for hours or days or weeks or however long this night had lasted. A party that had no end. Good times forever.

"Whoooo!" Ben shouted. There was more cheering. Someone tried to turn on a portable speaker.

"Oh man," the boy said. "Is it out of batteries already? How long has it been?"

The boy patted himself for a phone so he could check the time. But then he was caught up in the cheering too and forgot what he had been looking for.

Esther wanted to lie down, wanted to go back to sleep.

Or else to join them in their party, to forget herself in happiness. But she didn't. She was the only person left who was awake. There was no one else who could stop this.

She got up and looked at her brother one more time. He was dancing now, some other teenagers dancing with him. He had forgotten she was there. Above them, the moon sat where it been sitting since nightfall, where it would sit forever until Esther Gold put a stop to it. She watched Ben for one more moment, and then turned from the clearing and from the party, leaving the warm light of the campfires behind.

There was only her now in this bubble of frozen time. She took a breath, and then a step, and then another, and she was walking into the dark of the canyon until it swallowed her completely.

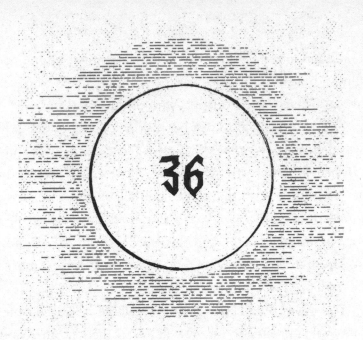

36

AFTER THE GLOW OF THE CLEARING, the dark
of the path was overwhelming. With the hills around her,
she couldn't even see the lights of nearby houses. She was
completely isolated in shadow. Even the sound of the party
behind her seemed to fade within seconds. Then it was only
her footsteps crunching on the dry dirt.

She continued forward, not letting herself hesitate. It
was like walking with her eyes closed. There was almost no
visual input. And every part of her body screamed at her
to stop, to turn around, and, failing that, to curl up on the
ground and cry. But she pushed through. She concentrated
on each step as it happened, not letting herself slow down.
If she slowed down, she would stop. And if she stopped, she
would turn back. And if she turned back, then they would
never be saved.

From the clearing, the path went along the stream. She knew that, and trusted her memory over the spirals and shapes her eyes made in the darkness.

Her foot almost slipped into nothing, and she had to lean backward to keep from tumbling into the stream. The path had split. One way went to the trail back up to the little park near her school. The other way went to the camp of the queen. Being careful about the drop-off, she shuffled her way to the left, toward the camp.

She heard movement on the hillsides to either side of her. She thought of what Aileen had told them, about the terrible creatures that lived in the Dream of Halloween, and how thin the separation between the two worlds would become the longer the queen held time where it was. This movement sounded like a huge four-legged animal, a wolf, or a lion, or some creature that did not exist in any form in her own world.

Keep walking forward. Concentrate on breathing. Here was a little wooden footbridge, beyond that was the entrance to the tunnel. On the other side of the tunnel was the camp. The orange light from the moon peeked out from behind a tree, and she could see the bridge and the tunnel tinted amber, like a flashback in a movie.

The movement in the hills behind her got louder, and she hurried onto the bridge. The moment her foot hit the first plank, the sounds of movement behind her stopped. She took a breath. It wasn't dark anymore, and nothing was following her. She was okay. She would be okay.

Click.

That insect sound. She knew what it was. *Click.* Then a sick buzz from under the bridge. A small hand appeared, gripping at the old wooden planks, and pulled the rest of its body out from under the bridge. It was the trick-or-treater dressed in a ragged pirate costume. Even though it was only a couple feet away, she couldn't see its face. The moonlight should have shone directly onto it, but somehow the face was in shadow. It clicked and buzzed. She screamed and ran the rest of the way across the bridge.

Once across, she looked back. The trick-or-treater was standing on the bridge, facing away from her, and making a scuttling sound like insect legs moving against each other.

Esther felt some impulse to try to reach whatever this creature was, even if her effort was hopeless. "You were once a child like my sister, right? Do you remember that? Do you remember being a little kid?"

The trick-or-treater turned. And for a moment, she clearly saw the face of a little boy, round faced, smiling, a distant memory of the person it had once been. And then its face was concealed in shadow again. The trick-or-treater clicked aggressively, but it didn't move toward her. It wasn't there to get her, but to block her way out.

Now the only way forward was through the tunnel. She had no choice. She couldn't go back if she wanted.

She had been dreading the tunnel the most. She didn't even like it when she walked home from school in the full brightness of day, and now it was a dark mouth waiting to swallow her. It might as well have been a portal to another world. She couldn't go in. She just couldn't.

Before she could do or think anything else, she walked into the tunnel.

Instantly she was cold, the air dropping in temperature from the already cool night air outside. Her feet scuffled against the leaves and trash that had collected on the tunnel floor. From where she was, she should have been able to see the other side, but she couldn't. It was like the other side was missing. She tried to walk faster. Her footsteps echoed unusually loud. The sound bounced back and forth, her footsteps repeating in front of and behind her, as if there were a whole line of Esthers marching forward together.

She stopped, and the echo in front of her stopped. But the echo behind her went a couple more steps before stopping. She held her breath, didn't move. In her ear, *click. Click. Click.* Insect noises. She shuddered, wanting to escape but unsure how. And then, on her hand, a tiny hand, human but cold. It brushed her palm.

She started running in the dark. Immediately she slipped and fell. Then she was up again, her knees aching from the fall, hoping she had her bearings right and wasn't about to slam into the metal wall of the tunnel. Behind her she heard four legs moving, an enormous predator on a hunt. There was a roar, like a tiger, but somehow metallic. Some dream animal, unlike any animal she knew, that had crossed between worlds to hunt her. And where was the ending of this tunnel? It had never been a very long tunnel, but she had been running for minutes.

Then the end of the tunnel came. She was back out into the night air, into the bright orange light of the moon. She whirled around to see what was chasing her, prepare for its attack. Behind her was just the tunnel, as it had always been. The entrance on the other side was completely visible, not far away. No otherworldly animals or faceless trick-or-treaters. Merely leaves and dirt and, barely visible in the dark, graffiti, scrawled and overlapping, years of bored teenage afternoons.

She was nearly at the camp. Turning away from the tunnel, she could see it clearly now. The tents and the banners and the burned throne. She still had no plan. She had come here because it didn't seem there was any other place for her to go. But what was here for her? A power she was no match for. A return to the Dream, or worse. She hadn't thought this out.

The stubborn instinct that had taken her through the darkness abandoned her, and she faltered, on the dim edge of the camp, one hand on the moon rock in her pocket. Perhaps she would have turned and run away, and let time stay frozen, let everyone sleep, given up. But before she could do anything else, a grease-smudged hand, big and calloused, grabbed her upper arm and yanked her toward the camp. From that point on, she had no choice but to face whatever would happen next.

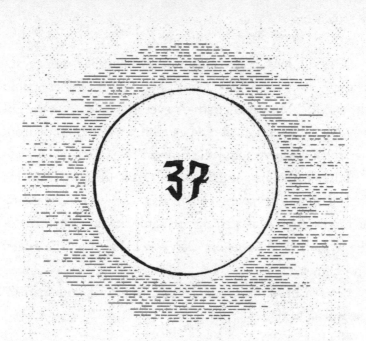

ED PUMKEN DRAGGED HER into the light of the camp.

"Found her sneaking," he said. "Little rat sneaking around." He didn't look at her as he pulled her, focusing only on the queen.

The trick-or-treaters, faces lost in shadow, clustered protectively around their queen just in case this was another distraction. Dan Apel sat sideways in the driver's seat of his truck, which was parked by the remains of the throne, watching intently but not making any moves yet.

"Very good, Ed," the queen said. "You've done well. Remind me that I should yell at you less."

"Yes, Your Highness," Ed said, diving into a kneel and pulling Esther over as he did it. She landed awkwardly on her side.

"Oh, Ed, look how clumsily you've handled our guest." The queen laughed. "You can let her go now. Where could she run to?" She caught Esther's eyes and made sure the girl was paying attention, and repeated it, all humor gone from her voice. "Where could she run to?"

Ed released her and went to stand next to Dan. He looked proud of having caught her, and he kept glancing at his brother as if waiting for some acknowledgment of the work he had done, but Dan was focused on the queen and Esther.

"So . . . uh, hmm . . . I'm sorry, what was your name?" the queen said.

"Esther."

"Right! Yes. Esther. I won't remember that. Seems unimportant. Anyway, girl, you've escaped the Dream. That's impressive. I don't think anyone's ever done that. Dan, has anyone ever done that?"

"No, Your Majesty."

"No. See? You've pulled off something that no one else has ever done, and you should be proud of yourself. I think it'd be good for your self-esteem. Take this time to really pat yourself on the back."

She winked at Esther.

"I mean, you don't have to physically pat yourself on the back if you don't want to. Whatever works for you. Stand there and glare at me like your mom told you to clean your room if you want. However it feels most natural to you to celebrate."

She leaned lazily sideways in the remains of her throne.

"But here's what I don't understand: Why didn't you just run? Did you want to achieve the world record for number of times escaping from me? Because it's good that you have goals, but I'll be honest, they're not realistic. Oh, I'm not just having fun, I'm actually curious about the answer. Tell me, girl, why didn't you run when you had the chance? Why come back into this canyon?"

"Where's my sister?" Esther said.

"Ah!" the queen said. "Of course. The sister. You want to rescue your sister. What a dull and human reason. I hope you brought an army that I haven't noticed yet, or have somehow gained a great deal of magic power, because otherwise this rescue isn't going well. Dan, show her how well her rescue is going."

Dan reached into his pocket. He pulled out a perfect red apple, the kind of perfect only possible through wax and pesticides, and rubbed it clean on his shirt. He tossed it into the air once, twice, and on the third throw it sprouted its razor blades. He approached Esther with the razor-studded apple. The blades looked deathly sharp, glinting an angry orange in the moonlight.

"Have an apple," he said, with a salesmen's false friendliness. "It'll be good for you."

Esther thought through her options. It didn't take her long to think through them, as she had none at all. So she took the moon rock from her pocket and held it above her head.

"I'll smash this," she said. "I'll smash this piece of the moon. I'll destroy it."

The queen held up her hand, and Dan stopped. The queen flashed an easy smile. "First off, smash it how? Destroy it with what? It's a rock. You throw it at the ground, you'll make more of an impression on the ground than the rock."

Esther didn't know. She kept it overhead, refusing to back down from the only stand she had left to make.

"Second," the queen continued, "the moon rock isn't technically the source of my power. It's an amplifier. It takes my power and just makes it bigger. I needed it to get things going, but now that time is stopped, I don't need the rock to keep it that way."

The queen held up a small, sharp stone that Esther recognized. "Remember this? A little piece of that same moon rock, broken off when your dentist friend stole it years ago. It seems that having this on his person protected him from the power I harnessed through the moon." She tossed the stone into the bushes and smiled. "But even that didn't save him for long, did it?"

The queen spread her hands in invitation.

"So if you can figure out how to destroy it, go ahead. As long as I'm here, the spell continues."

Esther tried not to believe her, searching around her for anything she could use that would damage the moon rock at all, but she didn't think the queen was lying. The queen seemed like someone so used to being in control that she didn't need to lie. And anyway, even if the queen didn't need the rock anymore, it still was obviously powerful, and ownership of it was currently the only thing Esther had over the queen. So Esther let her arm drop, still holding the rock.

"Oh that's too bad," the queen said. "I was excited to watch you try to hurt a rock for a while. But you *have* showed enough spark to change my mind. I don't think you're a job for Dan after all."

She made the slightest movement of her head, and the apple disappeared into Dan's pocket. He returned, whistling, to his truck. "Lucky break, kid," he said.

"Dan, you might think that," the queen said. "But I'm saving her for something better. I have a special corner of the Dream set aside just for her. A place with no illusions, no other people, only the raw material of the Dream and the Halloween moon to keep you company. I think you've seen it before?"

The queen cocked her head, and Esther felt a pull in her chest, like someone physically tugging at her heart. She saw a cliff of black rock, and an orange moon, and a deep, churning ocean. The queen was pulling her into the Dream. Esther tried to isolate where the tug was coming from, and she realized it was coming from her own hand.

"That rock can still be useful," explained the queen. "For instance, I can put a little of my power into it, and poof, it pulls you into a part of the Dream I don't think you'll find your way out of ever again."

Esther tried to fight the pull, but it wasn't physical, so she wasn't sure what to fight against. She tried to let go of the rock that had been turned against her, but her hand wouldn't unclench.

The queen sighed. "No, I'm afraid that rock is nothing special on its own. It was only the most convenient bit of the moon available at the moment. Just as you and this neighborhood are nothing special. I needed to do all this somewhere, and your town is . . . somewhere."

Okay. If Esther couldn't get rid of the rock, could she use it the same way that the queen was? Try to channel some part of herself through it. Channel what, though? Esther had no magic power, no special knowledge. She merely had a rock and a strong desire not to be put back into the Dream.

Alright then, she had a strong desire. Start there. Why did she have a strong desire to not be put in the Dream? Because she wanted her friends and family and life back. And why did she want that? Because she wanted to keep living and growing with them. She wanted to move forward with all of the people in her life, all of them moving forward in life together.

"None of this happened for a grand reason," cooed the queen. "You weren't plucked out by fate for some great purpose. You are merely a child, and this is merely a tedious slice of California suburb, and it was mere random chance that led you to this moment."

It wasn't working. The canyon was dimming. Esther could hear the waves. The pull had become more intense, and she felt like she was being turned inside out. She was almost in the Dream. If she was going to do something, she'd have to do it now.

She dove deeper into what she wanted, trying to find the core of it. She wanted to keep living. And that meant growing. And that meant changing.

Change. That was it. That was the heart of what she wanted. She concentrated as hard as she could on the desire for change. Because tonight she had experienced the opposite of change, and it was no way to exist. She took all of her desire to change, and she pushed it as hard as she could into the rock, against the pull of the Dream.

The world swooned back into focus. The sound of waves became fainter.

The queen's eyebrows shot up. "Are you fighting me? Are you actually fighting me? That's fascinating. I don't think I've ever had anyone try to match my power." She leaned forward. "I love it. Keep fighting. It makes this so much more satisfying."

Esther did keep fighting. She tried to clear away any fear, any doubt, any distracting thoughts or memories. She let go, for just a bit, of Agustín and Sasha and Mr. Gabler, of Ben and her parents and Grandma Debbie. She even, with difficulty, let go of Sharon. She only concentrated on one simple, pure idea. The desire to grow older. The desire to change. And while the pull on her did not go away, it also did not grow any stronger. She didn't seem any closer to the Dream.

"You are better at this than I expected," the queen said. "How amusing." But she did not sound amused. She sounded angry, and the human part of her voice was slipping away, revealing the voice underneath that sounded like metal striking metal. The queen stood, standing much taller than she had looked while sitting down, and she braced her body as though lifting a large and heavy object.

The pull in Esther intensified. It started to hurt, like she was being torn apart, but she kept focus on her desire to change, and directed that thought into the rock. As her options narrowed, she found that her thinking became clearer. The more desperate her situation, somehow the easier it was to focus in on this one idea. Maybe it was because there were no other ideas left that could be of any use to her.

"This is laughable," the queen said. She wasn't laughing. She was turning red, and her voice sounded like sparks and static. But no matter how hard she tried, she couldn't seem to fully send Esther into the Dream. Abruptly, the queen sat back down on her ruined throne, and the pull within Esther stopped.

"We've been looking at this the wrong way," the queen said. "I think maybe we got off on the wrong foot."

Esther couldn't speak. She was so exhausted by the struggle and weary of what the queen would do next.

What the queen did next was clap. One single clap, sharp but not loud. Every one of the faceless trick-or-treaters collapsed at once. Ed looked about in alarm, and even Dan frowned.

"Oh relax, you two," the queen said. "I've just borrowed back all the power I put into them. They're safe in the Dream for now. I'll retrieve them once I've dealt with this little problem."

She rubbed her hands together. The sound was like the crash of thunder.

"I don't want to start a precedent that a mere human can resist me and get away with it."

She held out her hands and closed her eyes. Esther felt something change. Some difference in her heartbeat or in the air. A soft wind against her face. She realized with a lurch of her stomach that time had started up again. The queen had dropped the spell for just a moment to concentrate all of her power on Esther.

The queen gave a small sigh. "I'll have to start everything up again once you're gone. You're officially very annoying. But that will only make this next part even more satisfying for me."

The pull returned with a jolt. This time it was violent and measureless. Esther's insides seethed. She tried to concentrate her thoughts on change again, to fight back the way she had before, but it was hopeless. Every thought was drowned out by the sound of violent waves and the eternal orange light of the moon. The gravity of the Dream as it drew her in became unbearable.

Then came a different sound, underneath the waves and the pounding of her own heart. It was a soft sound, but one that managed to cut through all of the noise. A meow. The tiny black cat came running across the camp, bounded up the arm of the throne, and landed claws first on the queen's face. For one last night, the Black Cats had returned. Aileen, despite herself, had joined the fight again.

The queen screamed. The little cat was a whirl of claws, drawing bloody scratch marks across the queen's cheek and tangling itself into her hair. Dan and Ed came running over but didn't know how to rescue the flailing queen without accidentally striking her. They hovered, waiting for some opportunity, too frightened of the queen's wrath to save her.

Esther felt the pull weaken as the queen was distracted. Esther couldn't waste the chance that Aileen was giving her. In that moment, Esther put all of her focus onto the rock. As she did, she felt the pull stop altogether, and then reverse. Now she was the one pulling. She was still falling into the Dream, it was too late to escape that fate, but she was pulling the queen in with her.

By the time the queen extracted the cat from her face and flung it into the bushes with a furious shout, Esther had fully entwined the queen with her focus. *I want to grow older*, Esther thought. *I want to change.*

The queen's eyes went wide.

"How dare you, you arrogant little

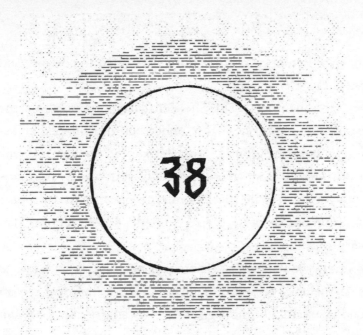

38

BRAT!"

She and the queen stood on the cliff, over the deep, churning ocean. The moon took up the whole sky. There was the dead tree next to them, skeletal branches flung up to the starless night.

"Well, great, look what you did," the queen said. "I hate black cats."

Esther found that the moon rock was still in her hands. The rock glowed a faint orange.

"I've escaped from the Dream before," Esther said.

The queen smirked. Here, in this strange and lonely place, the queen's regal dress seemed perfectly suited. Here was the context in which she made sense.

"You didn't escape anything," the queen said. "That rock let you out of the Dream."

"No. I stopped playing along. I decided to change. And the Dream let me go."

"Ha," the queen said. She didn't laugh, merely said the word. She tucked her dress under her and flopped cross-legged onto the ground. "You think force of will can break a dream? You think you just thought your way out of there, that you have some special brain no one else in town has? You're more stuck-up than I am, and, Esther, darling, I'm very stuck-up."

Esther looked about. There was nowhere to go. On one side, the black rock continued for as far as she could see, an endless plain with no sign of life, no landmarks at all. On the other side was the dizzying drop of the cliff and the horrible depth of the water. So she sat down on the ground across from the queen.

"I got you here, didn't I?" Esther said. "Trapped you in your own dream."

"Yes, you did. But again, Esther, I hate to tell you this. There's nothing special about you. It wasn't your power. It was the leftover bits of my power I had put into the rock. You used my own scraps against me."

The queen picked up a black pebble and tossed it idly off the cliff.

"You couldn't have forced your way out of the Dream no matter how hard you tried," the queen continued. "Every one of your successes has merely been because you were holding a magic rock, which is the silliest and saddest way to succeed. It's like a bad fairy tale. Even that rock wouldn't have worked if the cat hadn't jumped on my head at the worst time. Dreadful creatures."

"You're the one who started all those awful rumors about them."

The queen looked thoughtful. "Did I? Oh, you know, I might have. I've lived a long time. Done a lot of things. Anyway, to sum up, you're just a dumb girl lucky enough to be holding a dumb rock that I happened to put some of my power into."

Esther glumly examined the rock in her hands. She was trying to believe it wasn't true, but it made sense. Why else would she have been able to escape when Mr. Gabler and Agustín and Sasha were still stuck? What made her special? Nothing. The rock was special, even the black cat had been special, but Esther had just happened to be, as the saying goes, in the right place at the right time holding a magic rock.

"So what next?" she said.

"That's a good question," the queen said. "Ordinarily you'd be able to use that rock to leave again. But I'm currently using all of my power to keep you from doing so. Which puts us in an interesting situation. You need me to leave. I need you to leave. It's so annoying to need people. I hate it."

She pouted.

"But it isn't all bad for you, Esther Gold. Because it turns out we want the same thing. You love Halloween, I love Halloween. You and I both want life to be good forever."

Esther shifted the rock from hand to hand. The queen leaned back, looking up at the starless sky.

"It really makes no sense for us to fight, you know?"

"You kidnapped my sister. You put my parents and my friends into a dream."

"Esther, honey, details. I'll give you back your sister, how's that? I'll wake up your family and friends. I wouldn't want to deny you company in this forever Halloween. But think about it. You won't have to grow any older. You won't have to stop trick-or-treating. It will always be your favorite time of year, and you will always be the right age for the holiday."

Esther thought about it. She really did. She thought about Halloween, and about her family, and about time. She thought about her mother and father looking older every year, and what that meant. She thought about high school and then college and then whatever mystery lay beyond college. A wave crashed so hard onto the cliff that the spray floated up around them, hundreds of feet above. She tasted seawater in the air.

"There doesn't have to be a downside here." The queen spoke quietly and gently. "You get to have the people you love. Even that boy you like so much. And we both get to have Halloween forever."

In these words, Esther recognized herself. She had wanted to go trick-or-treating against the wishes of her parents and of Agustín, and so she had. Like the queen, she simply hadn't considered not getting what she wanted. Her love of Halloween, that had seemed so pure, felt tainted by the selfishness that she and the queen shared.

"Change is important. Change is good."

"Oh, Esther, you say those words like a child forcing down vegetables, but do you really believe them? Or are you just repeating what you've been taught, because that seems like what a good person is supposed to do?"

Esther didn't know the answer. She had been told that growing older and changing was good. But to her it still seemed terrifying. She shook her head.

"See?" the queen said. "You don't want to change any more than I do. And we don't have to. Together we can use the piece of the moon to leave this Dream, and then we simply stop fighting each other. Because we didn't have to, we never had to."

"This rock," Esther said, to the glowing piece of the moon in her hands. "It can take us back?"

"It's the only thing that can," the queen said. "You're lucky you have it with you. We'd be in a real rough situation without it."

Esther stood and stretched her legs and arms. She felt good. Or she felt okay. In any case, she felt ready. She held up the rock, and the queen smiled, getting up as well and brushing her hands briskly together.

"Great," the queen said. "You're making the right choice here."

Esther pivoted and threw the moon rock off the cliff as hard as she could. For a moment she could see it, a tiny orange dot against the dim gray glow of the sky, and then it was gone forever. The queen screamed, and as she screamed, her face transformed. There was a jittery and blurred shape behind the human face. Her scream sounded like hundreds of people screaming at once.

"You fool. You brat. You fool." The queen ran to the edge of the cliff and looked down, her hands on her cheeks. She whirled on Esther. "You terrible child. You have trapped us here. Do you understand that? Neither of us will ever be able to escape this place now."

"Isn't that what you wanted?" Esther said. "For nothing to ever change?"

"Not like this! Obviously not like this! Ugh, you take everything so literally. I hate talking to children." The queen had a red aura around her. She buzzed with raw power, and, without changing height, she somehow seemed to have become a giant. "I just wanted everything to stay nice. To live the good times forever. Not to be trapped in some dismal corner of this dismal Dream. But at least, little girl, at least I am trapped in here with you."

She moved toward Esther. Esther realized that the queen's feet were no longer resting on the ground, but dragged by her toes, as the rest of her floated. She seemed to no longer have full control over her body, the rage making her twitch. One of her arms went limp. Her forehead bulged and sagged. She didn't look like a human woman anymore, but like what she was—a hastily constructed imitation of one.

"Because, Esther—" Her voice was splitting, sometimes low, sometimes high, sometimes like a chorus, and sometimes like a child's whisper. It was falling apart into many voices. "Because, Esther, I will use every minute of every hour of every year of this eternity that I am trapped here on this nameless rock by a nameless ocean, making your life an endless, unchanging torment. I will introduce you to such pain that you will forget your name. You will forget everything but this present moment. And you will live forever in that present, wishing anything, *anything* could change, and nothing ever will."

Her face and body were blurred. She was mostly a cloud of red mist now. Her voice sounded like her tongue was formed from a swarm of wasps.

Esther watched all this, her hands going itchy and her face going sweaty. She had never in her life been so afraid. She had known there would be anger, but she had underestimated the depth and the shape of that anger. But she was comforted by the knowledge of what she would do next. She had known what she would have to do since the moment they had arrived in this terrible place.

"I used to not want change," she whispered. "I thought I didn't need it. But before tonight I thought Mr. Gabler was a boring nuisance, and now I know he's the bravest, most interesting person I'll ever meet. I hated Sasha Min, and she hated me, but that changed. That change was good. And the change between me and Agustín . . ." She wavered for a moment before finding it in herself to finish. "There is no life without change. In order for good things to happen in our lives, we have to grow older and change. Denying that would make me as selfish as you."

The queen laughed. She had no face anymore. Her laugh sounded like a boulder rolling down a mountain.

"And yet you gave all that change up," the queen sneered. "Now there will only be pain. Now there will never be anything different. Not for you. Not ever again."

"Well," Esther said, looking out over the swirling ocean to the broad orange moon that hung over it. The ocean sounded as violent as ever, water in constant argument with rock, and neither giving in. The red mist of the queen was inches away from her, some of the mist already wrapping around her wrist. She felt a sharp sting where the mist was touching her, the queen starting to deliver on her promise. Behind the queen was a dead, empty plain for miles and miles, maybe even forever.

"Here," Esther said, "is something different."

Esther Gold jumped off the cliff.

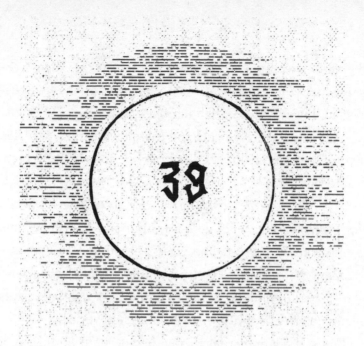

FIRST THE AIR. Whistling air. Howling, rushing air. Faintly in the moonlight, Esther could see the sheer black face of the cliff as a blur next to her.

Then the water. The moment before she hit the water, she saw a monstrous wave, almost as tall as the cliff. A mountain of water topped with a whitecap like snowfall. And then she was under, with a shock that spread across her entire body. She immediately plunged deep, terrifyingly deep. Well below the movement of the waves, to where even the orange moonlight did not shine, where all was still and dark.

A fall from that height, even into water, should have killed her. And maybe it had. She couldn't tell in the motionless, wet dark if she still had a body or not.

Gradually, she decided that she was not dead. She could

feel the water, brutally cold, pricking at her skin. There were things moving in the water with her, just as she had suspected, huge creatures. She felt one swimming next to her. The slow movement displacing massive volumes of water. Part of the creature brushed against her, and she felt frozen, leathery skin.

Shouldn't she be drowning by now? It had been a while since she had gone underwater. But air hadn't become a problem for her yet. She wasn't breathing, and for the moment that seemed to be fine. While it felt like water, and she floated in it like water, she didn't think this ocean was made of water. Not like water back in her world.

She saw a glimmer far in the distance. Up until then, it had seemed that all around her only ever would be dark. She had lost track even of which way the surface was. But she saw a bit of color and a bit of movement and swam toward it.

As she kicked her way toward the glimmer, she realized what it was. It was her. She was seeing her own life. Not like a movie projected on a screen, but more like a memory. The way that an image in our head can be simultaneously sharp and clear but also not actually there. She could see only the dark water, but also she saw herself. She watched herself, a year older, in high school. Not always happy, but making do. She wasn't alone as she had sometimes feared. In fact, she had a small group of friends, all of them going through the good and bad process of growing together. There were moments when she was generous, was kind, made good choices. There were moments when she cheated on tests, when she ignored people who reached out to her, or lashed out at people who didn't deserve it. Like life, she was both good and bad, a complicated mix that was impossible to sort neatly into either category.

The future she was watching skipped forward a couple years. She saw Agustín and herself, and they were both older, and she saw their hands clasped around each other. Holding hands. Walking. She saw lunches with Sasha Min, chatting and trying to guess what the test in the next period would be covering. Lunch after lunch, day after day, a friendship. She saw herself sitting in room after room, leaving each room a little older and a little different than she had entered it. High school and, past that, college. Which was still more rooms. More lessons. Different friends. She wasn't sure if Agustín was there anymore. The memory of her future was moving so fast now. It was a blur, like the face of the cliff as she had fallen.

She saw her family sitting in rows of chairs. They were all crying, and she knew that Grandma Debbie had died. But it was okay, her father was telling her. It was okay because death is part of the deal. If new people are going to be born, then older people must someday die. It was okay, but she still was sad, and being sad was okay too. Sadness is also part of the deal sometimes.

Now she watched herself graduate from college, the start of the rest of her life. No more rooms full of lesson after lesson. Instead, grown-up life was one long corridor, with only one lesson, which was how to make it from one end to the other. She looked different each time. She was always different. She was always still her.

The years moved faster. They whizzed by, with jobs that went nowhere and then a job that went somewhere, or seemed to, but that job ended unexpectedly, and then another so-so job that she took just because she needed a steady gig, and that ended up being the job she had for the next forty years. Evening hangouts with work friends, a house, bills, lots of bills, trying to understand tax forms. In all the motion and the passing of time, she couldn't clearly see who was with her, or if anyone was with her. She was so different now. She was decades older. Her hair jumped into different lengths and different colors. Her skin remembered her habitual expressions, bookmarking them in the folds of her face. Her face became a living record of all it had ever expressed.

And behind her, through all of this, she saw Sharon, who also grew older, who also passed through a series of rooms, a series of moments, and all of those rooms and moments added up to a life, and in front of her she saw Ben, and far in front of her she saw her parents, growing and changing too, until she didn't see them anymore, and she knew that they had stopped changing, and that the opposite of change was not stasis, but nonexistence. Eventually, her parents would stop changing, and that would mean they wouldn't exist anymore.

And then herself again, well into middle age. Nothing

about her life was what she, her thirteen-year-old self, would have wanted, precisely. But there was so much good in all of the changes that had happened to her. And also so much bad. It hurt so much, the growing and the years. But those years also contained every wonderful experience that had ever happened to her. The older her looked back to the younger her floating in the water. Their eyes met. Between them were decades of life and untold volumes of dark water.

The older her smiled at the younger her. And then the older her, which was really only one possible life that she could lead out of an infinity of possible lives, started moving farther away, drifting in a restless current. For a moment the younger Esther thought, *Let it go. I don't want it.* But even as she thought that, she was already swimming frantically toward it. Paddling and kicking with everything she had, until she was close enough to reach out her hand, and the older her, a woman older than her mother, older maybe than her mother would ever get to be—who knows?—reached out a hand full of deep grooves and creases, which was her own hand, and the two hands met, and she felt her head break the surface.

She was back in the canyon, neck deep in the runoff pond that marked the finish line of The Feats of Strength. Above her was the ledge she had never been able to jump off. She crawled, gasping, to the edge of the pond and pulled herself back onto land. As the water ran down her face, it did not taste foul or swampy, but alive and salty. It was not pond water. It was seawater.

40

"WELCOME BACK," SAID DAN APEL, leaning on his truck.

Esther stood at the edge of the queen's court, the water dripping off her clothes in such a quantity that she was immediately standing in a puddle of mud.

The moon was no longer on the horizon. It had moved slightly up and to the west, shedding most of its orange already. She could feel in the air and in her body that time was moving again for good. The endless Halloween night had ended.

She had half expected all signs of the queen and her court to have melted away, leaving only her unreliable memories to prove that what had happened was real. But no. Here was the huge camp, and the plants that had been knocked down and cut back to make room for it. There were clean-cut Dan and scowling, greasy-haired Ed, standing by their trucks. All over the camp were the trick-or-treaters, in their ripped and filthy costumes, with faces obscured in shadow. The trick-or-treaters were all sprawled on the ground, fast asleep. And there, on the burned throne at the center of the camp, was the queen. Also completely asleep.

"Yep, you did it, kid," said Dan. His nose was broken, and he had a black eye. "You trapped her in the Dream. Without her, none of this power holds. Your friends and all these kids will wake up soon. Isn't that right, Ed?"

Ed looked like he had gotten it even worse than Dan. His jaw was swollen, and there were puffy bruises all over his face, courtesy of Sasha and Agustín. He spat on the ground and grunted.

"Ed, that's disgusting. In front of a member of the public like that, even. Disgraceful." Dan gave her an apologetic smile, but his eyes remained cold and unmoving. "As I feel I will spend the rest of my life doing, I apologize for my brother. But the sentiment in general is shared. We're not huge fans of yours. I guess we could say we're enemies. But in defeat, I suppose it doesn't matter."

She watched the brothers warily, waiting for them to open up their trucks and unleash the weapons within. Dan caught her cautious glance.

"Oh, don't worry. Without our queen's power to back us up, there's not much point in us making a fuss. It'd be a heap of trouble for a fight that's already lost." He looked at the dreaming queen. "She had a lot of power, but no one said she was bright."

"Blasphemy," shouted Ed, balling his fists.

"Shut up, Ed." Dan appraised Esther, his face unfriendly but thoughtful. "No, she wasn't as bright as you. You are very clever. Me and Ed, we won't forget that. We won't forget *you*." He stopped a moment, narrowed his eyes. "If you ever decide you want to rule the Dream of Halloween, you just might have what it takes to pull it off. And I just might be willing to be your loyal adviser . . . and enforcer." He smiled his biggest customer-service smile and shrugged. "But in the meantime, we'll be out of your hair. Enjoy this victory while it lasts. Come along, Ed."

Ed spat again, to a disgusted sigh from Dan, and then the two of them started lifting up the trick-or-treaters and loading them into the trucks. Finally they approached the queen and carefully carried her onto Dan's truck. When they were finished, Dan tipped his hat to Esther and made a small, polite bow.

"Goodbye, Esther Gold," he said. "Keep my offer in mind."

He got into his truck. Ed was already waiting glumly in the other. The two trucks made their way out of the canyon. Dan switched on the mournful, warbling chimes of the truck, and the discordant waltz accompanied the vehicles back up onto the suburban streets and away into the last few hours of this Halloween night.

Esther stood in the deserted camp, uncertain what to do next. A young child sat up in his cot, blinking his eyes in confusion. He immediately started crying. Soon he was joined by another sleepy little girl, and then more children, all of them waking up from their long Dream.

"Sharon," Esther called, and ran over, scooping her sister up and holding her.

"Hi," Sharon said happily, not understanding what this game was but enjoying it. "Hi." She patted her sister's head.

Esther stayed on her knees, holding her sister for a long time, until she felt whatever inside her that had been broken by this ordeal come back together. This was the first moment since they had all been cast into the Dream that she hadn't had to face this night alone.

There were footsteps behind her, and she turned to see Mr. Gabler, Sasha, and Agustín groggily walking toward her. She shouted, no words, just a joyful sound, and ran toward them. She put her arms around each of them in turn, Agustín first, then Sasha, and then Mr. Gabler.

"You're all here," she said. It was all she could think to say. It was the best fact she had ever known. "You're all here."

"Yes," Mr. Gabler said. "Here but still trying to work out what is real and what isn't. I feel like I've been asleep for days. My back is killing me."

"Did we do it?" Sasha said. "Did we kick their butts?"

"No, Sasha," she said. "You kicked their butt. Man, I wish you could have seen them. Those brothers won't ever want to face someone like you again."

"Felt good to take things out on someone who deserved it, you know?" Sasha said, and smiled sweetly. Then she shouted, startling Esther.

"Edward!" Sasha grabbed her little brother from the confused and sleepy crowd of children. "Eddie, you're safe. I thought Mom was going to kill me."

"What about all these other kids?" Agustín said.

"Right, yeah, we should get them back to their families," Esther said, clutching Sharon's hand.

Mr. Gabler considered this, and looked around.

"Well, the good news is that most of them are patients of mine, so we can find out where they live. The bad news is that this is going to take all night. And from the looks of things"—he considered the moon, which was higher still, and the clouds rolling quickly over the stars—"that is way less time than it used to be. We should get started."

Esther took Sharon home. Sharon went happily to her bed, lay down, and, right before settling back into a completely unmagical sleep, gave Esther a big wink. For the first time, Sharon got it right, managing to wink with just the one eye. Esther winked back and turned off the lights.

THE LAST CHILD was returned to the last house, through doors left unlocked the night before to receive trick-or-treaters who never came, to parents who were still sleeping, but the natural and finite sleep of tired adults. Sasha was carrying Edward, who had fallen back asleep against her shoulder.

"Well, Esther," Mr. Gabler said. "Say hi to your folks for me."

She gave him a hug, squeezing as hard as she could to replace everything she wanted to express but didn't know the right words to use.

"I will, I will" is all she could think to actually say. "Thank you so much for everything."

"Oh sure, I mean, probably anyone would have done the same in my position."

"No," she said, letting him go. "I'm sure that they would not have. You're a wonderful man, Mr. Gabler."

He blushed. "Well," he said. And then didn't say anything else. He gave a little wave and walked to his front gate.

"Hey," Esther said. He turned.

"Yeah?"

"Ditch the toothpaste next year. Give out candy like everyone else?"

He thought about it for a moment. "Maybe sugar-free gum."

"It's a step."

"Good night, Esther," he said, and was gone.

Then it was just Esther, Agustín, and Sasha. They said nothing for a moment, unsure of how to say goodbye after their long night together.

"Sasha!" said a voice from the street. It was Mrs. Min, pulling up in the minivan. "Oh my god, Sasha. How late is it? I'm so sorry. I must have fallen asleep, and I didn't pick you up. You must have been worried. Were you worried? You must have been so worried."

Sasha handed Edward to Agustín, who took him uncertainly, as though terrified he would drop him, and she ran to throw herself into her mother's arms.

"Mom, I am so, so, so glad to see you."

Tears welled in Mrs. Min's eyes. "Oh, honey, you were so worried. I'm sorry I dozed off."

"It's okay, Mom. It's okay."

Edward woke up when he heard his mother's voice and

wriggled his way out of Agustín's hands to run up to the minivan. Mrs. Min scooped him up.

"Eddie! What in the world are you doing out of your car seat? What is going on here, Sasha?"

The Min family held each other. Soon Edward got bored and wriggled into the back seat where a couple of his toys had been left. "Vroom," he said as he moved a wooden airplane around in the air.

Mrs. Min noticed Esther and Agustín. "Oh, hi, kids," she said with surprise. "Sorry, I must look a mess, crying like this."

"Hi, Mrs. Min. Don't even think about that. We're glad you're here," Esther said.

"Do you kids want a ride? I know it's not far, but you could hop in."

"Yeah, we'll give you a ride," Sasha said.

Her mom gaped at her. "Sasha, I'm so glad to see you learning manners for once. And also making friends. You all are friends now?"

Sasha opened her mouth, but she looked at Esther and closed her mouth again, waiting for Esther to answer. Esther smiled.

"Yes, Mrs. Min, we're friends," Esther said.

Sasha broke into a relieved smile.

"I don't think we need a ride. But want to hang out tomorrow, Sasha?" Esther said.

"I would love to. I would . . . yeah. See you then. See you tomorrow."

Sasha helped her brother into his car seat, and then, with a last round of goodbyes, the Min family went home and now it was just the two of them. They walked in an easy quiet to Agustín's house. Like the rest of the neighborhood, it had reverted to its old self. The few gravestones in the recently mowed front yard each said "Sample" again. They went around the back of the house to his mother's workshop, where the lights were on. Through the window, they could see his mother asleep at her worktable, breathing slow and easy against a headstone with only the words "JOHN CARP" carved into it so far.

"She's safe," Agustín said. For the first time all night, he untensed his shoulders.

"She's safe," Esther confirmed.

"I guess you should go home," Agustín said. "Seems like a long time since we left our homes at the start of the night."

"It's probably been days, hasn't it? Weeks maybe."

"Only a few hours for everybody else."

"Who cares about everybody else?" she said. "Let's take a walk first. I'm not ready to pretend this didn't happen. I'm not ready to be with people who don't remember any of it."

"I'd love to. Where should we go?"

She took his hand. They walked down into the canyon. The darkness of it held no fear for her anymore. She knew what was in that darkness. It was the passage of time. It was herself changing. What was in the darkness was only the rest of the world, and she could handle the world.

They made their way up to the ledge where a couple

hours before—or maybe a couple weeks before, who knew—they had desperately tried to think of a way to free their friends and family. Now it looked like what it was, a bit of public park surrounded by cacti and the plant called mule fat. She laughed a little when she remembered the name, taught to her by her dad so long ago.

They sat on the grass and looked up at the moon, which was now in the center of the sky, small and white.

"I don't think I'll ever find the moon romantic again," Agustín said.

"You used to find the moon romantic?" she said, giggling a little. He rolled his eyes.

There was a pause. Neither of them looked at each other. She hadn't been alone with him since the Dream.

"When we were put into the Dream, do you think we shared a dream?" she said.

"Do you mean did we all have the same dream?"

"Yeah, or were they separate dreams? Were they like dreams we have normally?"

"You're asking," he said without looking at her, "if the version of the people you know in those dreams were actually those people, or just your own mind imagining those people."

"Yeah," she said. She turned and he did too, and they finally met each other's eyes.

"And if the things that happened for you with those people in those dreams happened for them too?" he said.

"Yes," she whispered.

"The house with the party in it," he said, and she felt her heart fizz into a joyful vapor.

"Two people going upstairs," she said.

"Esther Gold, I said it once in a dream, but I'm happy to say it again here. I like—"

She kissed him before he could finish his sentence. She didn't need to hear it. They had already told each other once, in a dream. Now she wanted this to happen for real, right now, here in this world. They kissed for a long time, and when they stopped they weren't friends. Friends was no longer the word for what they were.

For an hour, they stayed. They didn't talk. Occasionally they kissed. But mostly they watched time blissfully move, until the stars faded into the light blue sky, until the sun turned the clouds pink, until morning came at last.

ESTHER'S PARENTS WERE NOT HAPPY. From their point of view they had woken up on a normal weekday, in the early morning, to the sound of their daughter coming home. She had tried to be as quiet as possible, but her parents had been asleep for a long time and it didn't take much to wake them up.

"What in the world were you thinking?" her dad said. His hair was a mess, and his face was creased where it had pressed against the pillow. "I half expected you to sneak out for trick-or-treating, not that I'm happy about that, but then to stay out all night? On a school night?"

"Are you trying to punish us?" her mom yelled. "Is that what this was? You wanted to punish us by making us worry?"

She looked at her angry parents and felt such happiness

in finally seeing them again. She didn't know how to make her feelings match theirs. Everything they understood about the world was different than what she understood about it. So she just decided to be honest.

"It's so, so good to see you guys," she said. She hauled them into a big hug. "I'm so glad. I'm so glad."

Her parents looked at each other. Both of them were still furious, but it didn't seem possible to continue on their current trajectory given what was happening here.

"Are you okay, honey?" her mom said. "Did something happen?"

"You can talk to us," her dad said. "We're not that angry."

"We're incredibly angry," her mom corrected. "But you can still talk to us."

For a moment, Esther thought about trying to explain. She thought about telling the story. It wasn't a serious thought. It was only holding an impossibility in her head, just to see what it looked like, before letting it go.

"I'm fine," she said. "It was nothing. I'm just glad to see you. It's been a long night."

She held her parents for a while longer, not wanting to let go. They stood there, letting her hold them for as long as she needed. Finally she stepped back.

The velocity of their anger had been slowed, and there didn't seem to be much left to work with. Her dad sighed. "Well, you've still very much disappointed us," he said.

"You're grounded, I hope you know that," her mom said, but without much force behind her voice.

Their anger was renewed an hour later when Ben stumbled in from a party that had ended when the first light of the morning had shaken all of the high schoolers out of their reverie.

"I can explain," he said inaccurately.

Esther was glad to see her brother, and also glad to have her parents' anger directed at someone else for a bit. As her parents shouted, she quietly got her things together for school. By the time they were done, she was dressed, with the heavy backpack of textbooks on her back.

The phone rang. It was the police, calling to inform parents of the extent of the damages to the canyon. Not merely the little clearing where the teenagers usually partied, but a huge camp, entire bushes torn out and stomping down of the ground. There was even some kind of throne that had been half burned. The police department of such a quiet town had never seen a party of this size before, and they didn't like it. Esther's parents didn't like it either.

After that, the tone of her parents' words to Ben went up a notch, and Esther thought it was better to slip out. This all would be figured out eventually. As long as time kept moving, as long as everyone kept growing older, then eventually all of this would be in the past. She closed the front door quietly behind her and made her way to school.

AFTER

ANOTHER ORDINARY DAY of ordinary school. All this normalcy seemed totally wrong to Esther. The distance between this day and yesterday was life-changing for her, but for the rest of the world it was only another day.

As school let out, she and Agustín and Sasha walked out of the gate together, waving to Mrs. Min in her waiting minivan.

"All three of you today?" Mrs. Min said hopefully. Edward, in his car seat in the back, picked up one of his trucks to throw and then thought better of it, cradling the little car in both of his little hands.

"Actually, Mom," Sasha said, "I think we're all going to walk home." She started walking while her mom was still trying to recover from her shock enough to refuse, and so Esther and Agustín shrugged and followed after her. By the time Mrs. Min was opening her mouth to say, "Absolutely not!" Sasha was already in the rearview mirror, turning the corner to the street.

"Okay," Mrs. Min said. "Okay. Maybe just for today. Okay." She felt guilty about not picking Sasha up the night before, and so she wasn't ready for the kind of fight this was clearly going to be.

"Where do you even live, Sasha?" Esther said as they walked across the park. She and Agustín were holding hands, something they had done all day, to much comment from everyone in school. The general sentiment seemed to hover between "well, yeah" and "FINALLY."

"Carriage House Lane," Sasha said.

"Wait, really?" Esther said. "That's five blocks from my house. Why have I never seen you around before? And why was your mom trying to pick you up last night so close to where you live?"

"Well," Sasha said, "if my mom is so overprotective that she'll pick me up five blocks from my house, that kind of answers the question of why you never saw me around."

Esther let the subject lie, and they turned and started taking the long way home, the one that avoided the canyon. They had all had enough of that place for the moment.

"Speaking of which," Esther said to Agustín. "Is your mom okay?"

"Sleepy, but she can't figure out why. I told her that I think she's working too hard. I offered to help her so she can get stuff done in time, and in exchange we'll pick a

267

couple nights a week to hang out."

"Aww," said Sasha. "That's kind of sweet."

"It's very sweet," said Agustín. "I'm a sweet kid."

"So, high school next year," Esther said.

"Yeah," said Sasha.

"Yeah," said Agustín.

They were quiet for a minute. Kids from the elementary school went running by them, yelling.

"I think it might be fun," Esther said. "Or not fun, but..."

"But something big we get to do together?" Sasha said.

"Yeah, it's a big change, and it's a big change that we all make. That feels good. It feels good going into high school with a friend like you, Sasha, and..." She looked at Agustín.

"And a boyfriend," he said. "You can say it."

"Oh my god, I'm going to be the third wheel, aren't I?" Sasha said. Then she groaned. "I already am, aren't I?"

Esther took Sasha's hand with her other one.

"We don't have to make it like that. We all survived last night. We did it together. We'll do high school together too. Three friends."

Sasha squeezed her hand.

"I like that," she said.

"Two of whom also kiss each other a bunch," Esther said.

"Well, it started out good," Sasha said, taking her hand back.

"Like a lot," Esther continued.

"Okay, okay," Sasha said, covering her ears.

"I don't know what's bothering you," Agustín said. "All of

268

this has sounded great to me so far."

They passed adults in their driveways washing cars, walking their dogs, unloading groceries. Kids on their way home from school, excited to break into stashes of candy from last night. Not one of them knew what had happened. It was only another day of Southern California sunshine. The palm fronds on the trees along the street rattled in the wind, sounding exactly like rain falling. It was the closest thing to rain this town got for most of the year.

"Do you think we'll actually stay friends in high school?" Sasha asked quietly.

"Yes," Esther said. "I'm sure of it."

She wasn't sure, but she wanted to be.

"So are we going trick-or-treating again next year?" Agustín said.

Esther thought about it. She wanted to go trick-or-treating. But she knew that didn't mean she had to do it.

"No," Esther said. "I think I'm too old for that now. I'll find other ways to celebrate. Anyway, you don't like Halloween."

"I don't. But I like that you like it."

"I'm done with trick-or-treating forever," Sasha said. "I won't even let my kids do it when I grow up."

They laughed.

"Hey," Esther said. "Speaking of which, can we make a quick detour?"

The two of them followed her as she turned on to Meadowlark, down the street to Mr. Winchell's house. He was outside, prying the plastic gravestones out of the dirt. A pile of dismantled zombie dummies sat next to the side gate.

"Hi, Mr. Winchell."

"Hey, Esther," he said. "Sorry I missed you last night. I think I dozed off or something. I don't really remember. Had some wild dreams, though."

"It's okay, Mr. Winchell. But I wanted to ask you something."

"Shoot."

"Do you think I could help you decorate next year? It looks like fun."

He smiled and put his hands on his hips. "Well, sure. You'll have to ask your parents, but that'd be great, Esther. I'd be happy to teach you some tricks of the trade."

"That would be wonderful," she said. "That would be wonderful."

From there, life went on. Esther was grounded for a while. Then she wasn't. Ben was grounded for longer. Then he wasn't. Sharon wouldn't stop telling people about this weird dream she had, but no one could understand her description of it, and they all stopped listening. Mr. Gabler fixed teeth, and in the evenings he sat with Mrs. Gabler, watching entire seasons of TV shows at a time. Mr. Nathaniel washed his car and his sidewalk. On their walks home, Esther and her friends avoided him, crossing the street rather than getting close to the water from his hose. They never had learned who Mr. Nathaniel was, but if even the queen had been scared of him, Esther thought that she never wanted to know. Esther visited Grandma Debbie every weekend, even if Grandma didn't always recognize her. Esther would tell her ideas she had for new costumes, or the plots of horror movies she had seen, and Grandma Debbie would smile, and Esther felt that some part of her still understood. Esther's mom decided to go to graduate school. She was tired of being stressed about a job she didn't like. She wanted to be stressed about a job she liked. And Esther's dad sat down at a piano and started playing a song, a beautiful song he had never heard before, a song he was pretty sure he had written in a dream.

Esther Gold liked Halloween. She didn't love it anymore. She just liked it a lot.

Maybe you love Halloween. Maybe you dress up every year and put a lot of time and care into your costume. Maybe you watch scary movies and then can't sleep, but also can't resist watching more. Maybe candy corn tastes better to you than other candy, not because it tastes better (it doesn't) but because it tastes like a moment in time, like a season.

Maybe you think you love Halloween more than Esther Gold does.

And maybe you do.

Acknowledgments

Thank you to Meg Bashwiner and Jeffrey Cranor and Glen David Gold for reading early drafts of this book and giving good advice on how to make it a much better book than it was before.

Thank you to my parents Kathy and Ron Fink, who taught me a love of reading at an early age, and who took me to the movies on Halloween night so they didn't have to take me trick-or-treating. Thank you to my sister, Anna Pow, with whom I spent a childhood sharing and borrowing and discussing our favorite books.

Thank you to the Willapa Bay AiR program, which allowed me to sit in a little cabin on the coast of Washington for a month and write the rough draft of this book. It was a wonderful experience, and this book wouldn't exist without it. Check it out at www.willapabayair.org.

Thank you to the authors who I read when I was younger, and who taught me with their example how to write a book like this, most especially Bruce Coville, Jean Craighead George, Lois Lowry, Louis Sachar, Zilpha Keatley Snyder, and Jerry Spinelli.

Thank you to my editors Alexandra Cooper and Andrew Eliopulos, and the entire team at Quill Tree Books.

And, of course, a giant thank-you to Jodi Reamer, without whom none of this would be possible. Someday you and I will ride Splash Mountain, I promise.